Read Between the Lines

by

Sheila Kell

Coastal Investigation, Book Two

Read Between the Lines

Cover Art by *Lea Schizas*

The Wild Rose Press, Inc.
PO Box 708
Adams Basin, NY 14410-0708
Visit us at www.thewildrosepress.com

Publishing History
First Edition, 2024
Trade Paperback ISBN 978-1-5092-5376-0
Digital ISBN 978-1-5092-5377-7

Coastal Investigation, Book Two
Published in the United States of America

Dedication

To Janet Chalmers
I am excited you joined my beta readers. Your input
was invaluable to this book.
I look forward to continuing our work with Cassie and
JD's story.

Praise

"Wow! Can Ms. Kell tell a great story."
~ InD'Tale Magazine

"Sheila Kell is a mistress of the genre and she has a gift for crafting well-rounded, rock-solid characters and scenes that are emotionally charged and interesting."
~ Readers' Favorite

"What Sheila Kell does is create a series that would be intriguing to read and find out the story of every member of HIS Protection."
~ The Romance Reviews

Sheila Kell is the winner of three Readers' Favorite Romantic Suspense Awards, one Contemporary Romance Award, and has published fourteen books and one short story.

Chapter One

Killing is easier than I anticipated.

Of course, I only follow the instructions from the woman I love. She spells everything out so meticulously; I can't go wrong. Caring for my success, she also prepares and writes out how to avoid capture by law enforcement. I appreciate she loves me so much.

Finding the right victim is more difficult than strangling the woman. It's been a long time since I've been to a nightclub. Hell, I didn't realize they still existed. In my youth, I nearly lived in clubs, picking up willing women as often as possible. Little had I known this experience would assist me now.

Discouragingly, I waste three weekends finding the right victim. The victim must fit the description my love has dictated. The woman is petite—around five feet—with flowing blonde hair touching her butt and pure blue eyes. Why my love chose this type, I don't know—yet, but I will when she writes me again.

At the nightclub, I am young enough that my victim finds me suitably attractive to take home with her. With only one drink and a stupid one-liner which was written for me— "Are you a parking ticket? Because you've got *fine* written all over you"—she laughs and is putty in my hands.

My love is brilliant. To ensure I'm not captured on video at our victim's home, I pose as a security

1

specialist, which leads to a conversation about my victim's security. She, luckily, doesn't have a system but will listen to my pitch. *After* I see her place. Aka, a fuck first. The last part is not in the plan, and I can't improvise, but oh, how I want to indulge my hunger for a woman…my hunger for the hunt…my hunger for the kill.

No matter what my loins want, I won't cheat on the woman I love. Even if she never finds out, the guilt will eat at me. Some might wonder why guilt doesn't bother me for killing women. I have no answer, except she tells me to do it, and I love her.

One thing at a time. Again, I find the right woman who lives in a single-family dwelling—the best place to keep nosy neighbors away if she screams.

With my heart pounding, I keep to the shadows as much as possible when I follow the woman to her home, praying her neighbors don't have security cameras either. This is the tricky part and the part that could trip me up with law enforcement.

Inside her home, I cringe. The bedroom is all wrong. It isn't set up as my love demands—it should be pristine clean—but I can't do anything about the mess just yet. As before, I will correct the oversight after I've accomplished my mission.

My victim knows I want her. And, because I'm a man and she is beautiful and flirty, my cock shows the excitement of the evening. Maybe it is the upcoming kill that makes me hard. Either way, she notices and licks her lips, making my blood rush south.

I can't focus on that. Sex is not on the table. I must remember my instructions. Otherwise, I might fuck up and get caught with DNA.

As I come up behind the woman, the excitement in me thrives as she moves her hair to one side so I can access her neck. Instead of nibbling on the silky skin, I ask in a low voice, "May I tie you up?" I produce a red silk scarf in front of her. The blood-red color is a specific detail I must follow.

Hesitantly, she replies, "You won't hurt me, will you?"

Slowly, as I pull the scarf around her neck, I whisper, "Only 'til death." Then, I tighten the scarf. Of course, she struggles. Being prepared, I wear long sleeves and keep my head averted so her nails didn't dig in and grab my DNA. Any deviation could ruin things.

In reality—not TV or movies—it takes four to five minutes to strangle a victim. But only if enough pressure is consistently applied. A fighting, bucking woman makes it harder to keep the scarf tight. But I've prepared for this mission by working out and strengthening my muscles. So, I entirely close off her trachea in less than five minutes.

Disappointed, I wish I could have witnessed the essence of life flow from her eyes. Oh, the power to have in one's hands—life or death. My woman talks about killing many times, but I have not realized—until now—that she means for me to do her bidding. And I have. More than once already.

Continuing to prepare the scene for when she is found, Shawna—I think she said her name was—is stripped and maneuvered on her straightened bed covers. Thankfully, petite and thin equates to lightweight in my arms.

Before I get down to business, I put on gloves

Sheila Kell

extracted from my wallet and tidy up her bedroom. It isn't bad, just clothing she probably tried on for the evening out. I hang everything, sniffing her scent as I go. While not part of the plan, I can't help myself....

After setting the complete scene, I position Shawna with her arms out to her sides. The challenging part comes after I extract a knife from my pants pocket. I'm not squeamish with blood, but I'm not a fan.

Opening the knife, I lean over Shawna and slowly carve a cross over her heart. Nothing extravagant. Each line is approximately two inches in length. Once accomplished, I add the final piece. The one which shows I am my woman's willing puppet in these murders.

Almost salivating, I carve the number three on the lower right quadrant of the cross. Making the number readable is more complex than the "one" or "two" I carved into other women–too many curves in the number. I can't wait until number four when it will be lines again. My dick gets more rigid thinking about the next kill. The final kill.

Standing, I clean the knife on the sheets and survey the area to ensure I have left no prints or noticeable shoe tracks. Since we entered the home, I haven't touched a thing without gloves—nothing traceable that I was here.

I step out of the room, taking one final look at my handiwork, then shut her bedroom and the front doors. Once more, I remain hidden in the shadows until I reach my car. The walk is more terrifying than anything else. I may be seen, which would ruin everything.

The only thing left is to dispose of the gloves and knife which hold our DNA. I toss them at some point

4

on my trip home. Getting away with this crime makes me almost come in my pants. I lower the windows and allow the breeze to hit my face. Euphoria.

I know the woman I love isn't through with her murder list. I know it like I know the back of my hand. She is savage and bloodthirsty and will want more victims before it ends. And how will it end?

Chapter Two

Cassie McKay, PI extraordinaire, stood in the long line, smiling at what others said about her friend. In a matter of minutes, Missy Sauvage would be selling her newest novel, due to officially release tomorrow. Those who attended the Booking in Biloxi author event got the special treat of purchasing the book a day early. The affair brought authors from all over to showcase their novels, allowing readers to obtain signed copies and take selfies with authors and book cover models. But Missy drew a crowd each year because she showcased her newest release. While most authors in attendance wrote romance, Missy wrote straight-up suspense with only a touch of romance.

Cassie had read and bought all her friend's books, even though Missy insisted she get them free because they were friends. While she appreciated it, Cassie wanted to show support for her friend's work. It wasn't something everyone could do.

"I'll be the first to purchase *Cross My Heart*. Just try and stop me," one woman asserted to the other.

Cassie smiled. *Cross My Heart* being Missy's new release.

"Barbara Jo, you may think you'll beat me in line, but your fat ass is slow. You'll never catch up to me."

Uh oh. Things were escalating between the supposed friends at the front of the line.

"Fat ass," the first woman gasped. "Your ass is the same size, Janet."

Cassie scooted back as far as she could in the line and put her mind to Missy, who wrote well enough that friends would fight over her books. She and Missy met when Cassie had been a high school senior, and her mom had remarried and moved them to Louisiana. Being new at the school—without even a sibling to rely upon—Cassie had been alone, and only Missy had reached out to welcome her. The two became fast friends, but Cassie hadn't seen Missy in a long while. Since after college, when Cassie moved to Virginia for work, the two had never reconnected face-to-face. They had spoken via phone, text, and video chats, but this would be their first actual meeting in years. Cassie looked forward to it.

When the doors opened, Cassie hung back to avoid the crush of those rushing to Missy's table. While the readers would surely visit other authors' tables, they went for the gold first. Cassie joined the line to purchase the new release and was surprised when Missy and two men walked out, pulling her out of line. The evil glares she received almost made her laugh.

"Ladies," Missy announced loud enough for her long line to quiet and listen, "this"—she gestured to the taller of the men in a tailored suit— "is my agent, Robert Strong, who has helped me get this book to a publisher, and this"—she gestured to the other man in khakis and a button-down shirt— "as locals know is Carl Sperry, reporting for the Biloxi Herald. And this"—she hugged Cassie quickly— "is my best friend, Cassie McKay."

Okay, after working to be inconspicuous all her

life, this public outing made Cassie uncomfortable. She smiled nervously at the readers shooting daggers at her.

"Before I sell copies of *Cross My Heart*—sure to be a bestseller like *Hostage*—the person I dedicated the novel to gets the first copy."

Cassie stood stunned when Missy handed her the first copy of *Cross My Heart*—dedicated to her. What a fantastic honor and one not earned. Knowing it was too late to fight the idea—which is probably why Missy hadn't informed her—she hugged her friend, putting in a grip that showed the love she felt for her. "Thank you."

"I can't think of a better person to dedicate my book to. Now let me work this group before they revolt."

Cassie chuckled, relieved to be out of the spotlight. "You do it to yourself by letting them buy the book before the official release."

A smile tugged at Missy's lips. "Yeah, but it's more fun this way."

For the next hour, Cassie wandered the room, meeting authors of books she enjoyed reading, taking selfies with hot cover models, and purchasing books. She kept returning her haul to a spot Missy's assistant had allocated for her since she bought more than she could carry in one swoop. Maybe Cassie should have brought one of those wagons some women smartly towed around the event.

Cassie's heart began to pound when the suits arrived. The fun left the room with a silent whoosh. As a former FBI analyst, she recognized the look, the walk, and the overall persona of FBI agents. Had Mike—her asshat ex—sent this man and woman to hound her? He had made their divorce difficult enough amongst their colleagues. So much so that she decided a career change was the only option to get her life back.

Returning to Gulf Islands, where her mother resided, had been the first step to redeeming her life, and the second had been the honor of working at Coastal Investigation. Sure, one benefit was that her high school sweetheart was another investigator, her partner. He had all his friends deceive him a few months back, and they had killed one of them on their first case together, so things were not perfect.

When the agents descended on Missy and her entourage, Cassie rushed over, not wanting her friend hounded because of her. If Mike planned to play hardball, she would play right back.

Noticing Missy's distress, Cassie jumped into the fray. "I'm here. Why is Mike having you bother me? We're divorced."

The short man and tall woman turned to her and, if Cassie read them correctly, in bafflement. The woman recovered first. "And you are?"

"Cassie McKay, former FBI analyst, and FBI Special Agent Mike Rockwell's ex-wife. The female civilian you've come to hound. Don't worry, and it's not the first time. Although it is the first time since the divorce. I expect no less at this point."

The male agent spoke, "Ms. McKay, we're not here for you at all, and I take personal offense that you think we'd embark upon a personal spat with our professional office."

"This is great stuff," Carl murmured with his cell phone held out recording the conversation.

Feeling abashed and tiny, Cassie tried to

backpedal. "Well, it wouldn't have been the first time agents were sent to publicly embarrass me. If you're not here for me, then who?"

The agents looked at each other, but neither spoke.

"Me," Missy squeaked.

"You?" Cassie questioned. "Why?"

"They haven't said," Robert answered with a protective tone.

The male agent showed his badge. "Miss Sauvage, I'm FBI Special Agent in Charge Nick Angler." He tilted his head to the female agent. "This is Special Agent Miranda Miles." The female agent showed her badge. "Would you please accompany us for some questions?"

Cassie's mind whirled at the possibilities of their request. "I may have only been an FBI analyst, but I know you should be sharing more with her."

"Ma'am," Agent Miles said, "we've established we're not here for you, so please go about your business and leave us to ours."

The condescension sent Cassie's blood to boil. "Here's the thing—Missy *is* my business, and we're best friends, and I'm here to support her today. So, if you want to take her away, I plan to know why and make sure it's legal and not some FBI bullshit meant to scare an innocent."

The agents looked at each other again, which fumed Cassie's ire more. She continued, "So, why do you want to take my friend in for questioning?"

It felt like pulling teeth, but Agent Angler finally sighed and said, "Murder. We want to question her in the murder of Shawna Freeman."

"Wow." Carl's eyes widened, and greedy interest

blazed in them.

Damn reporters. "Well, that's simple," Cassie said. "Missy, did you know this Shawna or anything about her murder?"

Missy shook her head vehemently. "No."

"There you go. You're wasting your time."

"Oh, I don't know about that," Agent Angler said. "An agent bought your book this morning and read halfway through it already. And one of the murders matches our murder. And, since this happened recently, we will be taking Miss Sauvage in for questioning."

Cassie's head spun at the revelation, realizing the agents had not intended to share information but must have felt they were losing control of the situation.

"It's okay, Cassie," Missy said. "I'll go with them. I have nothing to hide, and I didn't do anything wrong."

This meeting felt all kinds of wrong to Cassie, and her gut twisted with anxiety. "Why is the FBI involved in this if it's a local murder?"

"Ma'am," Agent Angler said firmly, "if you don't quit trying to get in the middle of this, I'll have you arrested for impeding an FBI investigation." He turned to Missy. "Now, Miss Sauvage, would you please come with us?"

Robert pipped up, "I can keep things going until you return. What about an attorney?"

Cassie's mind was on other things. When exactly had this happened, and what was so familiar? All she knew was that this felt off, and her friend needed help. "Missy, do you have a local attorney?" It took her a moment to realize that was precisely what Missy's agent had asked, but she didn't care. It was an important question.

"No, he's in Baton Rouge."

"Okay, don't say a word until the attorney I hire gets to you," Cassie said, overriding what the agent had been about to say.

"It's okay. I didn't do this or anything wrong, let alone murder," Missy assured them.

Still, Cassie's distrust of law enforcement ran more profound than she would have liked, considering her past profession. "It doesn't matter. Just don't say a word."

Cassie watched the trio leave the event that had come to a standstill. This city was not her town any longer. How would she find a trustworthy lawyer for Missy who was available right now? The only attorney she knew had been the DA who had betrayed her boyfriend—it felt weird calling JD her boyfriend at her age.

She had to find JD. He would know someone, and she would not fail her friend. Cassie turned to the news reporter, agent, and PA, who stood as if waiting for something from her.

Shoving the phone from in front of her, she told Carl, "Enough of the interview with Missy." She turned to Robert. "I'll take care of the attorney since I'm local." She then turned to the PA, whose name she hadn't grasped. "I'll get my books later."

Although important in her life, books were well below the need to help her friend. She walked to her Jeep, ensuring the reporter hadn't followed her, and called JD. He would help. He always helped.

Chapter Three

JD Walker packed another box of kitchenware. He and his ten-year-old son, Henry Kyle, were finally moving from the boat to a home. Cassie had offered to help, but JD knew she wanted to see her friend at the book show. Not much of a reader, he never understood those shows. He read autobiographies, but they were usually of dead people, not someone you would meet in person.

"Dad?" Henry Kyle questioned. "Will I still go to Miss Pat's for school?"

Since his son had returned mid-year and had been previously home-schooled, Cassie's mother had offered to continue the school year for him. Being spring, the session was near an end. "For a bit more."

"Good. I like her, plus she's a better cook than you." Henry Kyle laughed and ran out of the galley.

JD loved the joy he saw in his boy these days. After Henry Kyle's mother's death, the boy had withdrawn. With counseling, things were coming along well emotionally for both. Henry Kyle still visited his counselor once a month while JD had finished counseling on preparing to be a single father.

After closing and taping the box, JD hefted it and carried it out of the small kitchen to the deck, where he had a pile ready to tote to his truck. He closed on the house in two hours. The sellers had cleaned and painted the place, allowing them to move in immediately.

His phone rang, and he pulled it from his cargo shorts pocket. *Cassie*. He smiled like he did every time he spoke with her. He had fucked up royally when they were teens and thought he would never have this opportunity again, and he certainly wouldn't screw it up.

"Hi, sweetie," he said upon answering.

"JD, I need help."

His panic rose. "What's wrong?" Had Cassie been in an accident?

"The feds took Missy in for questioning, and her attorney is in Louisiana. She needs someone right away. Who do you recommend?" she rushed out in one breath.

JD's hackles rose at the mention of the feds. As a former police officer, he had a love-hate relationship with the alphabets. "What for?" he asked as his mind whirled on local defense attorneys. The last two he had known best betrayed him, both willing to allow him to go to jail for a murder he hadn't committed.

"Something about her book and a murder." Cassie sighed loudly. "It sounds all kinds of wrong."

Anytime the feds took someone in, warning bells sounded for him. Who to call? He immediately thought of Lucy Collins but worried about what Cassie would say about his calling an old girlfriend. He couldn't think of anyone else. Not someone to tangle with the feds and a celebrity. They needed a pit bull, and Lucy fit the bill.

"Did they go to the Gulfport field office?" He wondered if he still had Lucy's cell number.

"I think so," she said. "I'm going to CI now to see if Gus knows anyone because he's not answering the

14

phone."

"I know someone." He headed below to round up Henry Kyle. He could square away an attorney, get to CI, and still have time to settle on his house. If they didn't move in this evening, so be it. They had survived the boat for months now.

"Thank goodness," she breathed out. "I know we work with some at CI, but I don't know any of them personally. I wasn't sure who to contact."

"I've got it. I'll meet you at CI." JD found Henry Kyle lying on his bed, headphones on, with his eyes closed. So much for his son packing his room. Then he looked around and saw the room all boxed up. The boy was ready for a bigger space.

JD tapped on his son's leg. "We've got to go." He turned and walked from the room, looking through the contacts on his phone. Yes, he had Lucy's cell number. Taking a deep breath, he pushed the call button. *Here goes everything.*

After three rings, Lucy answered. "JD, how are you?" she purred.

He used to love her purring out her words, but now it felt dirty. "Hi, Lucy. Are you available for a new client at the FBI office in Gulfport? It's Missy Sauvage."

"The author?" she asked excitedly.

"Yes. Something about Missy's book and a murder." He wished he knew more, but it was more important to get Lucy to the FBI office than for him to be knowledgeable.

"I can clear my calendar and get there in twenty minutes. I'll call ahead and see if I can stop the questioning. Hopefully, Missy is being smart and not talking with them."

JD heard shuffling in the background, probably Lucy getting her stuff together. "Thanks. I owe you."

"And I intend to collect." Lucy ended the call.

Damn, wrong choice of words. The two had ended when JD broke things off. Lucy had been getting clingy, and he hadn't been ready for a serious relationship after Susan's betrayal. Boy, oh boy, did he have friends who betrayed him. What kind of monster magnet had he been?

Lucy hadn't wanted to end things, and he hoped that when she saw him happy with Cassie, she wouldn't try anything.

"What's up, Dad? Is it time to buy the house already?" Henry Kyle asked as he caught up with JD.

"No, we're off to CI. Miss Cassie's friend is in trouble."

"Yay, I get to see Grandma Nan and Grandpa Gus. I don't see them enough." He hadn't brought his son to CI in the past few months, trying to focus on his work and Cassie. He and Cassie had not spent much time together because he had to build his relationship with his son first. Which meant the house came first today. He knew he'd said "So be it" if they didn't close today, but he wouldn't miss the appointment—no matter what kind of trouble Cassie's friend had.

JD and Henry Kyle quickly drove to Coastal Investigation and noticed everyone's vehicle, including Daisy's—the office assistant—in the parking lot. He looked at his watch. He had less than an hour and a half to fix this problem before the closing.

Walking inside, Cassie rushed to him and tossed herself into his arms. He enjoyed the warmth of her body against his. They hadn't made a secret of their growing relationship, and they had even found time to spend a few nights together when Henry Kyle slept at Gus and Nan's or Pat's.

"Thank you, JD. Whom did you call?" she asked as she pulled back. "Oh." She blushed and kissed him on the lips. A quick kiss, but still, she had remembered. "Sorry, I forgot that."

He held her tight. "Heck yeah, you did, and that's not a kiss." He pulled her back in and closed his lips around hers, molding them together, tasting her, and pulling back before he got too excited. "Better," he said.

Cassie laughed and swatted at him. "Let me go."

Reluctantly, he did. "Lucy Collins is on her way to meet with Missy and the FBI."

"Do I know her?" Cassie asked. Maybe she thought it was someone from high school or they worked with at CI. But it wasn't either.

"Uh oh," Daisy and her big mouth spouted.

Cassie narrowed her eyes at Daisy. "What do you mean?"

"It's just— Well, Lucy is one of JD's exes," the assistant said.

"With all the attorneys we work with, the first person you thought to call was an ex?"

JD could tell Cassie's temper began to spiral upward, and he didn't want to be downwind when jealousy ate at her.

JD's stomach turned. Yep, he may have created a monster problem for himself.

Chapter Four

Cassie's mind whirled with this new revelation. Did she have something to worry about with JD's ex? She shouldn't be jealous. Missy's situation should be at the forefront of her mind, but she couldn't help it. She was, after all, a woman in love.

"It's nothing," JD said. "Lucy is a pit bull, and we need a pit bull."

"She was the first person you considered?" Cassie asked, ire still rising. Why was she getting all upset? JD was hers, no longer this Lucy's. She took a deep breath. "I'm sorry. You're right, and this is about Missy."

"Good." JD eyed her warily. "I'm closing in a little over an hour, so let's see what we can find out before Henry Kyle and I must leave."

Cassie held up the book *Cross My Heart*. "It's got something to do with this, so I'm going to start reading."

"I'll read it for you," Daisy offered. "I'm a speed reader, and I can give you the highlights in less time than it will take you to read. Plus, you can make your calls."

Cassie stood, stunned. This was the first time Daisy had offered to do something for her. In the past, it had been a battle to get cooperation. Was the girl thawing toward her? "Um, okay."

"Besides," Daisy added, "I'm a big fan and have

read all her other books."

There it was. Cassie mentally shrugged. Well, it helped, so Cassie would take it. She handed Daisy her personalized copy. "Here you go."

"Thanks, Daisy," JD said. He turned back to Cassie. "Come on, sweetheart. Let's make some calls."

They bombed at finding out more about the murder the FBI wanted to speak with Missy about. They didn't know enough to tie the murder to a known multi-state killer. She and JD would have to wait until Missy and Lucy stopped at CI after Lucy rescued Missy from the interrogation. She hated it for her friend. Cassie had seen what a Rottweiler her ex-husband had been and knew some FBI agents were more ferocious.

Still, they needed a pit bull. She shook her head at the dog references. Cassie only hoped JD was right about Lucy.

"I've got to go," JD said. "Are you gonna be all right without me?"

She smiled at his thoughtfulness. He worked so hard to keep her happy, and she wondered if she reciprocated enough. "Yeah, I'll be fine. I'm excited for you." Finally, he and Henry Kyle would have four walls that didn't bob in the water.

"I am, too." JD turned to his son. "Come on, champ, let's go buy us a house."

"Woo hoo!" Henry Kyle yelled. "I'm getting a big room painted blue."

Cassie smiled and said goodbye to them. She looked around the room. Daisy read the book. Gus and Nan watched the door behind JD and Henry Kyle, frowning.

"What is it?" she asked the couple.

Nan looked at her. "Nothing." She turned and walked away, and Gus followed her. What the heck? She couldn't guess what their frowns meant, so she put it from her mind. Missy was her worry.

Cassie knew a few feds from her days with the FBI, but she refused to call her ex or his friends, so she called Levi. Like her time with the feds, he wasn't an agent but could find out anything. Pulling her cell from her pocket, she found his number and pressed the call button.

Levi answered after one ring. "Hi, kiddo. Do you miss me?"

She did miss him and hearing "kiddo" from the older man. Since her first case with JD, she hadn't spoken with Levi. Months. Boy, was she a horrible friend to only call when she needed something. "Hi, Levi."

"Are you ready to marry me yet?" he jested.

"Anytime. You know I'll be ready," she joked back. In her mind, she thought of how Levi and her mom would be great together. They were around the same age. They were both a bit eccentric. And they were both great people.

"What do you need?"

"Why is it I need something?" She did, but still, for him to assume meant she had been bad at communicating with him.

"You only call when you need something. Don't get me wrong. I don't mind."

Feeling guilty, she told him, "I do need a favor. My friend, Missy Sauvage, is being questioned by the FBI in Gulfport. I want to find out what's happening, but everyone here is tight-lipped. There's something about a murder."

"The author?"

"Yes, the author." She was proud of her friend's popularity and hoped it didn't make things worse for this case.

"Let me check on a few things, and I'll get back to you," he said and disconnected the call.

Cassie went to her desk and sat. What to do now? She decided to get on Amazon and read the description of Missy's new book and see if any early readers had posted reviews because that might help her understand more.

She cycled through and noticed Missy's book was already #1 on Amazon's bestseller list, and *Cross My Heart* hadn't even been released to the public. No reviews, though, since it was not live for reviewers, so she would check BookBub and Goodreads later to read the early reviews from readers who received an advance copy of the book. Cassie read the blurb. Wow, Missy had some imagination.

Missy's book described a serial killer committing murders as the author wrote the novel. Daisy would be able to tell her why and how. She peeked over at the assistant, who was almost finished reading the novel. Amazing.

Her phone rang. *Levi.* "Hello again."

"Hi, sweetheart," he said. "Boy, oh boy, do you get into tangles."

"What do you mean?"

"A new serial killer is operating in Mississippi and Louisiana, killing the same as in your friend's book."

Cassie's mind spun. "So, maybe she wrote from real-life experience—it happens." Had Missy not had an original idea? The thought disappointed Cassie, but if Missy took the book to a new level, excellent on her.

"Yeah, but her book just so happens to include something the FBI left out of their public information," Levi said.

"Finished," Daisy said. "You're not going to believe this."

Cassie shook her head at Daisy and held up a finger to forestall her. "What do you mean?"

"Well, the fact the killer carves a cross in their heart has been released, but not that he puts the number on their chest and where it is specifically located," Levi told her. "Along with the fact it happens exactly like Ms. Sauvage wrote the scene in her novel."

Cassie's heart sank to her stomach like a stone. "What are you saying? Do they think Missy did this and then wrote about it?"

Levi paused too long for Cassie's liking. "I'm not sure what they think, but it is mighty coincidental, and FBI agents don't like coincidences. Anyhow, that's all I've got, kiddo."

"I appreciate it, Levi," she said, and the call ended.

Daisy came up to her. "Do you want to know?"

Did she? Cassie shook, thinking the FBI might consider her friend a serial killer. She had a rundown from Levi on what the feds had, so Cassie should listen to what caught their attention in her book.

Daisy gave her a cliff notes version of the book reiterating what Levi told her. Cassie wondered whether Missy had heard what the FBI kept quiet or whether she imagined it for her book because her friend would not murder anyone.

She heard a vehicle drive on the white shells lot

outside. Cassie jumped from her chair to the front door, hoping it was Missy. In walked her friend and a tall, slender, beautiful blonde goddess who could have been a supermodel. Cassie was glad she had dressed up and put on makeup for the book show; otherwise, she would feel frumpy around this woman.

The woman Cassie presumed was Lucy looked around the office and frowned. "Where's my JD?" Just like that, Cassie decided her friend needed a new attorney—pit bull or not—and quickly.

Chapter Five

After his closing, JD looked at the house keys in his hands and relaxed. He owned a home but could not forget the accompanying mortgage. But, at thirty-six, he was finally adult enough to be a homeowner. Elation filled JD at the thought of him and his son in a non-floating home. However, he would never give up his sailboat.

Looking at Henry Kyle, JD smiled. "Ready, champ?" They were still at the title company after signing away the next thirty years of JD's life. He wanted to get them to the house and unload the boxes from the truck before it rained.

"Yeah, Dad. Are we going to our new home or back to work?"

Work. He had forgotten all about Cassie's friend's problem, and he knew to keep that fact to himself. Should he go by and see how things were? He should, since Lucy had most likely brought Missy back to CI by now.

"Are you okay if we stop by work to see how things are, then go to our new home?" He hoped the rain would hold off long enough to check on his woman. Yes, his woman. He loved her with everything he had in him.

Henry Kyle grimaced but nodded. "Sure, Dad."

Which JD took as not really. He had to put his

family first, and Cassie knew and understood that. Henry Kyle had been through a great deal over the years, and he needed stability, and home was stability.

"Okay. We'll go by the house first, unload, then run to CI before we pick up pizza for dinner." He knew the pizza would do the trick.

"Let's go," Henry Kyle encouraged as he headed out the door.

JD chuckled, said goodbye to the realtor and closing agent, and followed his son to his truck. Yep, it was still loaded. Their furniture would not be delivered until the next day, but Henry Kyle wanted to sleep in his room the first night, so air mattresses it was.

They breezed through town with light traffic and arrived at their new home. JD looked at the brick house built twenty years earlier. He had wanted something newer to avoid repairs upfront since his savings nearly emptied for the down payment. Luckily, this home had new appliances and systems, so he considered it a win.

"Well," JD looked at Henry Kyle, who removed his seat belt, "how does it feel riding up to our own home?"

"Good, Dad," his son said, jumping from the truck.

JD sat momentarily with the heaviness of fatherhood and the joy of homeownership resting within him. He grew up in a broken-down trailer and was called "trailer trash" for most of his adolescent years. Never would someone call his son that. They had a nice three-bedroom, two-bath home that should withstand the storms. He glanced at the roof, recently replaced since the last hurricane. At least something will survive.

Watching Henry Kyle wave him toward the front

door, JD exited his truck and tossed the house keys to his son. Sure, he wanted the pleasure and satisfaction of opening his new home for the first time. But his son was so excited, JD decided to give Henry Kyle the privilege.

"Thanks, Dad."

"Do I carry you over the threshold?" JD said jokingly.

Henry Kyle made a horrified face. "Heck no."

"How about a piggyback ride, then?"

His son moved his head around as if thinking. "Okay."

JD loaded Henry Kyle on his back—boy, how his son was getting heavy and a bit old for this.

They held their breath as Henry Kyle reached around and turned the key in the lock. *Their own home* still beat within JD's mind and heart. When the door unlocked, Henry Kyle asked, "Ready?"

JD would miss sleeping on the deck of his boat, the bobbing in the water lulling him to sleep, but this was better for his son. "I was born ready."

"That's so old."

JD laughed. According to his son, Henry Kyle found most of his sayings "old."

They laughed as they bounded into the home. Henry Kyle squirmed off JD's back after they crossed the threshold.

The house looked so different empty. When they looked at the home before purchasing it, the rooms had furniture and pictures on the walls. It had looked homey. Now, it mirrored a bachelor pad.

Well, they were bachelors, after all.

"I'm going to see my room." Henry Kyle strutted

down the hall. The good thing was that it was a split design, and JD's bedroom was on the opposite side of the house from Henry Kyle's. It was perfect for when Cassie stayed over.

JD did a quick walk-through to ensure all was well, then went to the truck to unload the boxes. They didn't have many since the boat had little space. They needed a big case at CI, where the client paid a bonus, so he could spoil his son with things JD never had as a child.

Henry Kyle rushed out and rooted around the boxes, looking for his. He lifted one and headed inside.

JD shook his head. "You know there are more boxes out here," JD shouted to his departing son's back.

"I know," Henry Kyle said as he returned for his second box.

JD unloaded the rest while Henry Kyle set up their air mattresses and sleeping bags. The boy was excited about camping inside.

As JD finished, he thought again of Cassie and her friend's dilemma. He was damn curious about precisely why the FBI wanted to question a fiction novelist.

"Ready to head to CI, champ?"

"Then pizza?" Henry Kyle flashed a big smile.

JD chuckled. "Then pizza."

"Can we get cheesy breadsticks too?"

"Sure." His mind had already switched to Cassie, and she wasn't happy with him about hiring Lucy, even though she finally said it would be okay. He had to make it up to her.

Arriving at the CI office, he noticed an abundance of vehicles. Good grief, everyone and their brother were there. When he saw Lucy's Mercedes, he sighed at the thought of seeing her again but rejoiced at her pulling

Missy from the clutches of the FBI.

When he walked into the building, the tension hit him like a sledgehammer to the gut.

"Darling, there you are," Lucy said as she approached him, all smiles.

He glanced at Cassie, who looked narrow-eyed at Lucy. *Uh oh.* He had to do this right. "Hello, Lucy," he said but walked past her to Cassie. "Hello, honey." Then he leaned down and kissed her luscious lips.

"Well, I never," Lucy said behind him.

Cassie looked up at him and smiled sweetly. "Thank you," she whispered.

He had no idea what she thanked him for—Lucy as an attorney or the kiss. He would go for the kiss. "You're welcome." He winked and turned back to the group. Seeing a female he didn't know, he reached out his hand to her. "You must be Missy. A pleasure to meet you."

Missy grinned and shook his hand. "It's all my pleasure. I hear I have you to thank for Lucy's help."

He glanced at Lucy—who had crossed her arms over her ample chest—then back to Missy. "Just helping out my Cassie." He reached for Cassie's hand and held it in his. He wanted no misunderstandings with this group about his and Cassie's relationship. He loved her and would do anything for her.

JD nodded as Nan and Gus took Henry Kyle to the backroom.

"Now," JD said. "Tell me what's going on."

Chapter Six

Cassie beamed at the attention JD showed her in front of that Lucy woman...her name for the attorney. Sure, she had been ecstatic Lucy had rescued Missy from the FBI, but the woman acted as if JD were hers. *Jealous much?*

"Let's sit," Cassie suggested to the group after Robert and Carl entered and were introduced.

Missy explained the writeups Carl would complete for the local newspaper–this case would be included. Cassie didn't like the reporter there, but it'd be okay if he kept out of CI business.

Knowing Daisy was a fan and Cassie still needed to build bridges with the young woman, she said, "Daisy, you'll want to join us."

They moved to the conference table in the center of the room. Cassie smiled when JD scooted his seat closer to hers. Sure, it was a childish thing, but it worked.

That Lucy woman scowled at them, and Cassie didn't care.

"Let's start with you, Missy," JD said.

"I'm not sure where to start, but I'll go with my book."

"*Cross My Heart,*" Daisy piped in, "wherein your antagonist kills off characters through strangulation, then carves a cross over their heart and numbers them, but it is happening while the protagonist author is writing a novel about the same type of murder."

Missy smiled. "You read fast."

Cassie about fell to the floor at Daisy's blush from the compliment.

"I'm a speed reader," Daisy said.

JD shifted in his seat. "Okay, tell me about today."

"Today," Missy began, "I was selling one-day advance copies of my book. It doesn't officially release until tomorrow, but it's a promotion the publishers put on for this event."

Most of those at the table nodded. That Lucy woman looked bored, checking her perfect manicure. Carl, who also seemed bored, took notes or doodled. Cassie couldn't tell. Robert had his eyes on Lucy–poor chump.

Cassie wanted to smack the group and tell them to pay attention, but everyone seemed to know what happened and were waiting for something new.

"The FBI showed up and asked me to accompany them for questions. Since it didn't seem I had a choice, I went with them."

"Mistake," JD said. "At least without a lawyer."

Missy nodded. "I get that now."

"So," JD said, "what does this have to do with you?"

Missy sighed. "A serial killer is using my book's MO on their victims, right down to the numbers. The killer is one shy of the final number in my book."

Silence reigned.

Cassie wondered out loud, "Could you have heard of the murders and used it for your book?" That would explain things happening while Missy wrote the book—

just like the protagonist.

Carl perked up at that suggestion. He stopped doodling and watched Missy.

Missy looked appalled. "No way. I completely made up the plot."

"Coincidence." JD sighed. "Police hate coincidences."

"Well, they had released the strangulation, and the press found out about the cross carved across the hearts, but no one knew of the numbers or the author bit except law enforcement," Cassie added.

"When did these killings happen? Did they say?" JD asked.

Missy nodded. "Since I started writing my book."

Just like in the novel. Cassie didn't like the coincidence either.

"Maybe someone read your book early?" Daisy asked.

Missy shrugged. "Some people read it early—my editor, my beta readers."

"I didn't read it until it was finished," Robert said, now watching Missy instead of the attorney.

That took him out of the running, but Cassie knew not to make any judgments until she had proof of their innocence or guilt.

"What are beta readers?" JD asked.

"Oh," Missy said, "they're specific readers who read the book early, sometimes a chapter at a time, and give feedback to help improve it. They might tell me something does or doesn't work, and stuff that helps me make the book stronger."

"Could one of them have done it?" Cassie asked. It had to be one of them unless... "Has the book been pirated yet?" She added "yet" because it would be at some point. Some thought authors didn't deserve to be paid for their work, but authors spent all their time writing and spending money publishing and advertising. The small royalties were their living income and paying bills after the expenses.

Missy shook her head. "It hasn't been pirated yet. My editor and beta readers have been with me for years, so I doubt they'd suddenly act out my novel."

"That doesn't mean anything," JD said. "We'll need the names and contact information for your publisher, editor, beta readers, and anyone else who handled your book since you began writing it."

Missy nodded.

"Do you want to keep Lucy on retainer?" JD said, and the attorney brightened.

"I'll gladly do it. I love going up against the feds," Lucy boasted.

Missy looked at Cassie, and Cassie nodded. May as well keep the pit bull on staff. At least on retainer, she wouldn't be around every day.

"That would be great, Lucy," Missy said.

"Great. Tell me more about your antagonist," JD instructed.

Missy gasped. "I didn't think—"

Daisy piped in. "In the book, it's a beta reader who committed the murders, thinking the author is telling him what to do. But, unlike the ones Missy says she has, the antagonist was a new beta reader."

Cassie had not heard that part and wondered why no one had said it before now. It was a downright freaky coincidence. "So, a beta reader? What about your editor?"

"My editor is Victoria Callahan, and she wouldn't hurt a fly," Missy insisted. "She wouldn't turn into a murderer just to make my book more popular or chance putting my reputation in jeopardy."

"People will surprise the hell out of you," Lucy said. She stood. "Listen, if you don't need me any longer, I'm out of here. I have other clients." She turned to Missy. "I'll have my assistant send over a contract." Then she turned to JD and gushed, "Bye, sweetheart."

As that Lucy woman left, Cassie realized she didn't say goodbye to anyone else. She heard Daisy, under her breath, mutter, "Bitch." Those were Cassie's sentiments exactly.

"Ignore her," JD said in her ear. "She's just jealous of you."

Cassie smiled. She was, wasn't she? Cassie couldn't remember anyone ever being jealous of her, and she liked the feeling, even though it was immature.

"Now," JD said, "let's get those names, numbers, and addresses. Missy, provide Daisy with as much information as possible about these people. How many are we talking about?"

"That read it before the first murder? Four—my editor read the first three chapters in the beginning, which had the first murder, and didn't read the entire book until I finished. My three beta readers read as I write, one chapter at a time," Missy said. "After the novel was complete, the entire production team had access."

"It's a place to start." JD stood. "I promised my son pizza, and by gosh, I'd best get it. Cassie, are you coming by to see the new digs?" She had already seen the house as he had dragged her along while home shopping. She had been searching for herself, but not as diligently as he. Things were fine at her mother's home for now.

"Of course," she said. "I can't wait." And she could not wait to see the home that might one day be hers also. She was getting ahead of herself. They had only been back together a few months. However, those months had been fantastic.

They were in love, once again.

Chapter Seven

Lying on an air mattress the next morning, with his hands behind his head, JD contemplated marriage. It didn't frighten him as much as before he reconnected with Cassie. He'd never been opposed to marriage, but he hadn't considered it, even with his long-time girlfriend Susan. Oh, Susan had talked about marriage more than once, but JD had never seriously entertained the state of matrimony with her because he had never loved her the way he had loved Cassie in his teenage years.

With Cassie, marriage felt right. They'd been meant for each other. Yet, it was too soon. They'd only been back together for five months. Not enough time to jump into marriage. Plus, he still had his son to worry about. He had no idea how Henry Kyle would feel getting a new mother figure in his life. At some point, JD would have to ask and avoid his son resenting a woman who took on the stepmom role.

First, they had to figure out how to uncoil Missy's problem with the FBI. He could understand their interest in her, especially after hearing about the book. It was identical to real life. Had someone decided Missy wanted them to murder people like in her novel? It seemed far-fetched, but JD knew it had to be one of those four. Second, the editor had only read about the first murder. Unless Missy lied about knowing of the homicides and used them as her plot. Cassie believed the storyline had been completely fantasized by Missy. JD wasn't so sure. Yet, how would she have known all the details—enough to write about? That was where he got stumped in the investigation.

Henry Kyle raced into the bedroom and launched himself on JD's large air mattress, bouncing as he did.

"Whoa, champ," JD said, moving his arms back to balance himself. "Where's the fire?"

Henry Kyle laughed. "Dad, you say some of the oddest things."

JD frowned. He hadn't thought it odd or outdated. "What do you want?"

"Can we go to the beach today? It's Saturday, and I don't have school."

JD would love nothing better, but they had a furniture delivery to deal with, and he knew Cassie would be elbow-deep in the case. "Not today. We've got the furniture, and I've got to go to work. Hey, maybe Miss Pat will take you." He realized his mistake in volunteering the woman without consulting her. Heck, he didn't know if she was home to watch his son. He rubbed his forehead. This father stuff had been tougher than JD had expected.

"Yes!" Henry Kyle pumped an arm in celebration. "Do you think she'll want to go parasailing?"

Ever since the two of them had parasailed, the boy asked to go almost every day. The kid loved being in the air. Maybe his son would become a pilot. "I doubt she'll want to do that. How about just playing in the water and collecting shells?" Henry Kyle began collecting odd or different shells. He didn't have many, but his son was proud of his collection.

"Do you think she'll go in the water with me?"

JD was still wondering if Pat was home and available as they built out the day. He'd hate to disappoint his son. "I'll tell you what. Go get dressed and brush your teeth while I shower, and we'll go to Miss Pat's." JD would call her first to ensure she would help.

Henry Kyle rushed from the room.

"Don't forget to brush your teeth," JD yelled after him.

Well, so much for a lazy Saturday. At least he'd spend most of the day with Cassie. Collecting his phone from the floor, he called Pat, and she assured him she'd love to take Henry Kyle to the beach. Cassie's mom was a gem and a lifesaver. He really had to find a regular sitter, so he didn't need to rely on Pat so much, especially since Henry Kyle's aunt had moved up north for a job. But those problems were for another day. Today was about furniture, Missy Sauvage, and her damn book.

After a quick shower, he wore his traditional khaki cargo shorts and a black T-shirt. Sometimes he wore long pants to work, but clients had come to accept his laid-back style. Plus, he'd finally gotten Cassie out of those uptight business suits. She'd donated many of them to the local high school for students prepping for interviews. She had such a kind heart.

Grabbing his wallet and keys, he asked loudly, "Son, you ready to go?"

Henry Kyle rushed into the room—the boy seldom walked—in his swim trunks and a T-shirt with some anime character on it. JD should know the character, but the name escaped him. The standard headphones were around his son's neck. The boy couldn't survive without them. "Ready."

JD shook his head. "Did you remember to get a towel to dry off with?"

His son turned and bolted down the hallway, presumably searching for a beach towel.

Looking at his watch, JD's mind returned to Cassie and marriage. When he finally decided to propose, how would he do it? He'd want it to be a special and memorable occasion but not cliché.

"Ready, Dad," Henry Kyle said breathlessly.

Checking to confirm he had a beach towel, JD led the way to the front door. After they exited and locked the place, they climbed into his truck and headed to Pat's cottage. He smiled at his new house as he drove by. It was good to be a homeowner.

He felt the need to build his son a fort. All boys needed a fort. JD never had one, but over many years, he had tried to create one with dead tree limbs he'd gathered from the property. He'd wanted someplace he could escape his father. Only, he hoped Henry Kyle used it for fun and not as a need to escape.

Arriving at Pat's, she stood on the front steps of her cottage, beach bag in hand. The woman was amazing. He hoped he was as spry at her age. Although she wasn't very old.

"Hello, Henry Kyle," she greeted. "The beach is calling."

"Huh? I don't hear it?" Henry Kyle responded.

JD shook his head. The boy took everything literally. JD would have to work on that to ensure his son wasn't made fun of when he finally attended traditional school. "She means it's time to go."

Henry Kyle looked at his dad. "Well, why didn't she just say that?"

JD started to respond, even going so far as to open his mouth, but decided against it. "Have fun," he said instead. To Pat he mouthed, "Thank you."

She waved her hand as if it was nothing. "We'll enjoy ourselves. Now, you go get furniture, then help Missy. I always liked that young lady."

That was his plan. Only how to do so stumped him.

Chapter Eight

Early morning, I sit with the rolled newspaper in my living room. I like the feel of the paper in my hands instead of reading it on a device. I can't give up old habits.

After a sip of coffee, I briefly look around the room and know I need to make a change. But why would I at this stage? Eventually, Missy and I will be together and live in her grand house or my Mississippi home. I'll never bring her to this shack in Louisiana. She'll pity me for living like this while our love grew.

Turning back to the newspaper, I unroll it and immediately spot the article I expect—*FBI questions NYT's bestselling author.*

"Fucking FBI!" My voice reverberates around the room, reminding me of my loneliness.

They are going to screw up everything. Missy will stop writing, which will ruin our connection. It took me so long to realize she spoke directly to me in her writing. So, in *Cross My Heart*, I finally acted on her story. She was even specific that it was a beta reader who should commit the crimes. How more straightforward did she have to be to realize the story was meant for me to play out?

She always wanted me to be the villain wreaking havoc in the world and beefing up the publicity for her books. I don't mind being her puppet. I love and admire her more than life itself.

One day, I will tell her my work for her, and she'll fall more in love with me. I only need one or two more books to bring to life, all for her sake.

The scene on Friday at Booking in Biloxi shocked me. Too many people butted their noses into what should have been an easy interview with the FBI. I could ensure the FBI didn't bother her too much. My mind whirls on possibilities to hinder their interference.

Chuckling, I guess the FBI arriving and hauling off their star author wasn't the publicity the Booking in Biloxi people wanted. But they don't matter in the scheme of things. They were just a conduit to Missy and I finally meeting face-to-face.

And she was more beautiful than the pictures on the back cover of her books. Honestly, I've watched her a few times before the event. I wouldn't call it spying since we're in love. Oh, how I love her with my entire being. We are made for each other.

As for the investigation, I know the feds will never believe Missy killed those people. So, I don't worry about that. But what if she mentions my obsession with her work and that she spoke directly to me, telling me to do those things? No. She also knows we need more books to establish her as the best in the writing world— a consistent #1 *NYT's* bestseller before she can devote her life to me.

I can't be the only one to have a love for her literary talents. No, she isn't at the top yet. But with my help, she would be that and more. The more people know her name, the more books will sell, launching her to the top of the charts.

Since I finally realized she spoke to me, maybe she

wants me to go back and act out her other books. Hmm…

Taking a sip of coffee makes me wonder how Missy takes her brew. It hasn't been revealed in all the interviews she's completed. I've read or watched them all. I tried to find out, but she didn't take coffee yesterday.

Sure, my psychiatrists tell him I obsess too much over things and that I need to step back sometimes. Missy isn't one of those times. I don't care what the shrinks say. They never seem to understand love and necessity. I love Missy, and making her a star is necessary. She can be my obsession, and then I'll be hers one day.

In the news story I read, there is speculation Missy didn't create the plot. Some say she copied it from real life and is a fraud. I toss the newspaper down on the living room table and surge from my seat on the couch. "How can they think such a thing?"

Stressed, I pace back and forth in my living room, my fists on my forehead. Now and again, I hit myself, not hard, but enough to hopefully jolt an idea into my mind. Have I screwed up? No, I couldn't have messed this up. She told me what to do—step by step.

How could they think she copied my work? I didn't act out the scenes until she showed them to me. Surely the feds would figure that out. But what about the public? I can't turn public sentiment away from her. It was precisely the opposite of the plan.

What to do? What to do?

Things were so twisted.

In a saner moment, an idea comes to me. I stride to my second bedroom, transformed into a home office, and sit at my computer. I'll send Missy a note to tell her what to do this time. It is time I speak to her. Hopefully, she'll listen.

After several attempts at what to write, I look at the final draft and nod. Yes, this will do. I read it out loud before printing it. Donning gloves from the kitchen stash for when I handle meat and jalapeños—plus my kills—I add a single sheet of paper to the printer and print the note.

My dear Missy,

Don't let the FBI scare you. You must keep writing. It took me so many years to read between the lines and realize you told me what to do—for our sake. You must keep our secret. Don't let the feds weasel it out of you. We have so much more to do. So many more wrongs to right in the world. I will forever do your bidding.

All my love,

Your ardent fan

Yes. It will do. I use an envelope with a tear strip, so I won't have to lick it and leave DNA. After affixing a self-sticking stamp, I pocket my gloves to dispose of them elsewhere, grab my keys and wallet, and leave the tiny home. I'll mail it from New Orleans. Somewhere busy, where they can't tie it to me.

Satisfied with my plan, I drive away, whistling a happy tune.

Chapter Nine

On a gorgeous Sunday, the wind whipped through Cassie's hair. She took a deep, pained breath and sighed. "I feel guilty being out on the boat while Missy is in trouble."

JD checked the sails and tightened a rope. "There's nothing we can do right now except talk through the case. We can discuss the case here just as well as on land."

This trip to Ship Island with Henry Kyle had been planned for weeks. She understood that JD does not want to disappoint his son. She didn't want to, either. She also didn't want to fail her friend.

Henry Kyle poked his head up from below. "Are we there yet?" he asked with his headphones pushed back on his head, just off his ears so he could hear the response.

Cassie mentally shook her head. She barely remembered the boy without the headphones lately. They may not have been an ideal present from her mother. The boy had wanted them so badly that Pat had bought them for him for Christmas.

"Not yet." JD walked to his son and removed the headphones.

"Dad," Henry Kyle whined.

"No, you're going to socialize with us," JD directed.

Henry Kyle huffed, crossed his arms over his chest, and said, "Okay." He wandered over to the bow of the boat with Cassie. "What are you talking about? Let me guess—work."

Cassie raised her eyebrows. The boy was extremely smart. They had been talking about Missy's case. "We were," she said, "but we can talk about something else."

"Okay," Henry Kyle said, "are you two getting married?"

Cassie almost spit out the sip of the drink she'd just taken. Her gaze caught JD's and he smiled.

"Not today, champ."

Today? JD insinuated he had considered it. Her heart expanded with her love for this man and his son. She couldn't wait to be his wife but presently was too soon in her mind. She understood they should wait, which sounded like JD did, also.

"Look," Cassie said, pointing to the water around the boat. "Dolphins."

Henry Kyle ran to the railing. "Look, Dad. They're swimming with us. Whoa, look at this one jump." He laughed, glowing with happiness. "Did you know that dolphins are mammals, and they swim in pods, not schools like fish?" he asked without turning his gaze from the dolphins.

JD's and Cassie's eyes met with merriment. The kid was learning a great deal from her mother in homeschooling, and he was always willing to teach everyone else what he'd learned.

"I did," JD said. "What else can you tell us about them?"

Henry Kyle turned around and held up his hand,

one finger at a time. "They are warm-blooded. They breathe through the lungs and not the gills. They have live births—yuck." Henry Kyle made a disgusted face. "Their mothers make milk—double yuck." He shuddered this time. "And they have body hair."

"Hair?" Cassie asked jokingly, knowing they did, although one wouldn't believe they did.

The boy turned to her, and his eyes widened. "Yes, they do." Then he scrunched up his nose. "At least that's what your mom told me." He turned to his father. "Dad, do you think Ms. Pat was funning me?"

"Funning you?" JD asked with a smile. "No, champ, she wouldn't do that. Supposedly, they do have body hair. Now, come here and help me steer her into the island."

"We're there already?" the boy asked. Then he nodded as if answering his question. "That's right. It's only twelve miles off the coast—meaning, it wouldn't take long to get there."

"We're not there yet," JD told him. She didn't think JD would allow the boy to help him pilot the boat near the pier or anchor offshore with the many tourist and excursion boats and ferries in the water around the small island.

"What else has my mom been teaching you?" Cassie asked before she took another swallow of raspberry-flavored carbonated water. After trying the beverage, she'd become addicted to the flavor and dumped her diet soda.

Henry Kyle shrugged. "All kinds of stuff." He turned to his dad. "Can I pet the dolphins?"

JD reset the Saints ball cap on his head. "May I?" he corrected his son. "And, yes, you may try. Hold your hand out and see if one will jump close under it. On the way back, we'll stop and see if any swim up to the boat."

Henry Kyle leaned out, scaring Cassie, even though he wore a life vest. JD didn't seem as worried. The boy held out his arm as far as it would reach. He waited and waited and while a dolphin had come close, none had been close enough to touch.

"Look," Cassie said, "I see the island."

"Whoo-hoo!" Henry Kyle shouted, jumping up and down, disappointment at not petting a dolphin forgotten. "Finally."

"Did you put on your sunscreen?" JD asked his son.

Henry Kyle sighed. "Yes, Dad."

"What are you most interested in experiencing?" Cassie asked the youth, attempting to keep his spirit high.

Excitedly, he rushed out, "I want to see Fort Massachusetts. Did you know it was built in the 1850s to protect the coast?"

Growing up here, she knew about everything about the island, including the owner, although she'd never met the man.

The pier was full of paid charters, so they anchored the boat offshore and swam to the island. JD placed their cooler with water and snacks inside a life ring and floated it to shore. With the heat and sun, they would dry in no time.

Today promised to be fun for the three of them. Despite feeling guilty for not helping her friend, but if she focused on Missy's troubles, she wouldn't enjoy the day to the fullest. JD was right. They couldn't solve the case now, so fun in the sun it was.

"Come on, you slowpokes," she said behind her as they swam to shore. "Last one there is a rotten egg." Then she laughed as JD passed her with his son on his back.

****

JD should have reminded Cassie to put on sunscreen. He could see the redness on her face and arms. Not a severe burn, but enough to irritate the skin.

They'd had an enjoyable time on the island. JD's son wanted to stay longer until he was reminded they might spot more dolphins on the boat ride home. It had pleased him to see his son interested in history while touring the old fort. It had been part of Cassie's and JD's Mississippi history class taught in the ninth grade. The schools no longer taught the course, but it appeared Pat held onto the desire to teach about our state history. He couldn't appreciate the older woman any more than he already did.

They swam to the boat and climbed aboard. After putting on a dry T-shirt, JD went below without a word to the others. When he returned, he handed a bottle of aloe vera gel to Cassie. "Here, you'll need this."

Smiling—JD loved her smile—she said, "Thank you," and accepted the bottle.

"Miss Cassie, did you get sunburned? I could have given you some of my sunblock. It was SPF one million or something like that." Henry Kyle rolled his eyes.

She laughed. "I would have taken you up on it."

"Dad," Henry Kyle said, "are we going to play with the dolphins?"

"Well," JD said as he prepared to launch, "we might even get to swim with them."

"Yippee! Did you hear that, Miss Cassie? We might swim with the dolphins."

"Come here, champ, and help me with the sails."

Henry Kyle stood tall and put his hand to his forehead in a salute. "Aye, aye, Dad."

"Get over here, you rascal."

The boy laughed and raced to help JD set sail to return to the coast.

When JD saw a pod of dolphins playing, he steered the boat near them, until they swam alongside. He swiftly lowered the sails and cast anchor, allowing Henry Kyle to leap off the boat with Cassie. JD prepared the vessel to remain in place while they swam.

JD could hear Henry Kyle's laughter as he dove into the chilly water. After breaking the surface, he quickly searched for his son and smiled while treading water, just as a dolphin showed off for them. Keeping his son in sight, JD swam to Cassie. He noticed her eyes were on his son. JD loved and appreciated how she looked after Henry Kyle like a mother would. She would make a great stepmother. No, he hated the word "step." She'd be a great mother, period.

It took all his willpower not to pull her into his arms and allow her to float on his lap. But they had Henry Kyle to watch. Fear suddenly churned in his gut as his son grasped a fin allowing the dolphin to drag him along on its swim. Knowing the dolphins in this area were used to humans, JD's gut was unclenched, but he couldn't allow his son to get too far away. He winked at Cassie. "See you in a bit." And swam toward Henry Kyle. "That's far enough, son. Let go."

Henry Kyle immediately did so. JD was thankful his kid was obedient. His ex had done something right while raising him.

He caught up to Henry Kyle, whose life vest kept him afloat. "Race you back to Miss Cassie."

"Okay." Henry Kyle stroked toward the love of JD's life.

"Hey," JD joked, "you got a head start."

"I'm a kid. Of course, I get one." Henry Kyle continued swimming with all his might to beat his dad.

JD coasted behind his son, ensuring the boy was safe and the kid won the impromptu race.

Nearing Cassie, Henry Kyle asked, "How come I'm the only one who has to swim with a life vest on? I'm a strong swimmer."

"You are," JD said. "But you're not experienced in the ocean waters further from the coast where a wave can drown you. Once you get more experienced, I'll let you remove the vest." Over his cold, dead fingers, JD thought. His son could wear it until he was fully grown as far as he was concerned.

As Henry Kyle climbed aboard, JD swam to Cassie and gave her a quick, loving kiss. "I miss those lips."

She smiled, and his heart swelled with love. He should ask her to move in with them, but how would his son take it? He should discuss this with him first.

"I miss yours, too," she responded.

After they were aboard, JD set sail for home and the work to be done. Although he'd told Cassie not to think about the case today, he had considered it several times. To help her friend, they would step on the FBIs toes, and it wouldn't be pleasant. He only hoped Cassie's bastard of an ex-husband didn't turn out to be part of the equation.

Chapter Ten

Of course, Cassie's bastard of an ex-husband had to be involved. Since the murders were multi-state—Mississippi and Louisiana—the agency sent a small task force. *Lucky me.* JD got to meet Mike McKay in person. He hoped to keep from punching the asshole in the face for hurting Cassie.

Bright and early Monday morning, Agents Angler and Miles entered with a rather good-looking man with a broad build and short military-style haircut. Agents Angler and Miles stood on each side of the doorway while the other man removed his sunglasses as he boldly walked into CI. McKay. Why did the man have to look like he'd been on a magazine cover? Couldn't he have been some homely guy she had only loved for his personality?

In his expensive suit that reeked alpha male, Mike McKay strolled into Coastal Investigation on the presumption of telling CI to step down and leave the investigation to the professionals—the Federal Bureau of Investigation. JD knew the asshole was there to check on, and bother, Cassie. One night, Cassie had expressed how Mike and his friends had made her life miserable before, during, and after the divorce. JD would *not* allow the prick to cause any more misery.

After informing JD, Cassie, Nan, and Gus that the FBI was handling the case and CI should drop it, Mr.

FBI special agent-extraordinaire pulled Cassie aside for a private word. Worried for Cassie's mental health, JD followed and put his arm around her shoulders, pulling her close to show his possessiveness. A high school move, he knew, but he didn't care at this point. McKay would not abuse Cassie with his words.

"JT," Mike spat, "I said a private word with my wife."

"JD," Cassie corrected, but McKay didn't break eye contact with him.

"Ex-wife," JD corrected at the same time. He knew it was a stupid caveman power trip, but neither man wanted to look away first and show weakness. He tried to teach Henry Kyle that hate was a strong word and dislike should be used unless hate was truly warranted, and that should be few and far between. Well, JD hated Mike McKay with every fiber of his being.

Cassie slipped from under JD's arm and slid between the two men, with a hand on each man's chest.

While JD watched her through his peripheral and knew her by her scent and presence, he didn't look away from the asshole in their midst.

McKay broke eye contact to look down at Cassie with the venom in his eyes he'd directed at JD. When they didn't soften, JD almost reached across the woman he loved to tear McKay apart, limb by limb.

"Look," Cassie said, "this stuff won't happen." She didn't specify "stuff," but JD could guess it was the dominance thing, and JD had that in spades. So did McKay, but JD knew he could take the agent. It wouldn't be pretty, but who cared about pretty when someone deserved a beat down. He mentally shook his head. JD wasn't violent by nature and disliked that

McKay brought that personality out of him.

Gritting his teeth, McKay said, "I just want to speak with you alone. We don't need a— chaperone."

Cassie turned. With her back to JD, he couldn't tell if she searched the prick's eyes or what. But then she turned to JD. He wanted to smile looking at her slightly sunburned face, remembering the fun they'd had together as a family. He wished they could have extended the trip into today to avoid the bastard and asshole of the year.

"It's okay. I can handle him," Cassie said with pleading in her eyes.

JD wouldn't second guess Cassie in front of the royal asshole, but his gut said, "Don't leave her alone with McKay." Against his better judgment, JD told her, "Okay, but I'm here if he steps out of line."

McKay bowed up his shoulders at the comment. "What kind of man do you think I am, JT?"

JD knew he said the name wrong to show he was unimportant in McKay's world. JD also stood tall and drilled his gaze into the asshole's. "I know exactly what kind of man you are. And, if you hurt Cassie one more time, you'll answer to me."

Cassie sighed loudly. "Boys, boys. Stop this."

They both looked down at her, and JD's gaze softened. His woman was tough. He knew that. She had changed since they'd been back together. She'd regained her courage lost during the divorce and subsequent mistreatment by the asshole. She could handle anything. However, JD still didn't want to leave Cassie.

"I'm okay. Truly," she said.

It took nerves of steel to nod and walk away, but

not so far that he couldn't respond immediately if he noticed Cassie's demeanor change to one he disliked. Or, if he saw McKay's attitude change. JD didn't trust the man, and, by God, he hated to admit it, but he was jealous of him. Not the man, but the years he'd had with Cassie. The years that should have been for him-had his dad not royally fucked up their lives.

As JD moved aside, he wondered if this was how Cassie felt around Lucy. It wasn't like he had been married to her, but he had been in a relationship with her. Plus, Lucy was a sexy woman who used her charms how she could.

"*Cher*," Gus said to JD, "she be fine. Cassie be a strong *femme*."

JD knew that, but still, it was her royal asshole ex-husband they were dealing with. "I know, Gus. It's just—the man isn't good for her."

"Come now," Nan added, "we're all right here. What would he do?"

Probably toss out horrible words. JD shrugged, trying to focus on Nan and Gus—the owners of CI and his bosses—while keeping an eye on Cassie and McKay. "You're right. What's the plan today?" he asked, knowing Gus would eventually defer to him for what the day held for them, but it was always good to make the man feel important. Since Gus and Nan had stepped down as primary investigators, JD had noticed Gus was a bit down in the mouth. The man needed to be involved, even if it was just a bit. JD would ensure it happened in his case. He wanted the man happy, and he was certain Nan did also.

Gus looked at Cassie and McKay, then back to him and Nan. In his best Cajun-English, he said, "You go see those readers Missy has. They be suspicious."

JD's exact sentiments as well, especially since they were the only ones to read along as she wrote the novel, plus the murders occurred not long after they were written, precisely as she'd penned. This was damn suspicious in his book, the only suspects he could consider now. Yet, it was early in the investigation, and he'd previously learned not to choose the villain before he had the evidence. "I agree. Cassie and I will take the readers, but I think you should also speak with the editor and agent. They might have some insight into the readers for us." There, that would give Gus a task that wouldn't be too stressful. JD noticed Nan's slight nod and smile at him. So, she knew Gus needed a job to keep him occupied. Good.

Glancing at the door, JD noticed Agent Angler looking uncomfortable as he watched McKay. Why? Was he upset at McKay taking over? JD would have been if it had been his case.

Turning to look at Cassie, to see if she needed him, JD thought about asking her to move in again. Was it too soon? He still hadn't spoken with Henry Kyle. Having a kid in the mix, maybe it should be marriage first. But wasn't that too soon also? He mentally shook his head. It was all so confusing. Life with a kid, that was.

McKay spun around and walked away with the agents on his heels. JD looked on as Cassie watched her ex-husband leave the building. She bit her lip, which he had learned was her serious thinking giveaway. What was going on in that brilliant mind of hers?

Cassie shook her head and turned, her gaze locking with JD's. After connecting, the curiosity and fury in her eyes softened. Now he had to know what her conversation with McKay had held. He needed to know what her ex had said to have put that fury in her gaze.

As she walked to the group, JD touched her, grasping her hand. He had to remind her he was there for her, no matter what. Plus, he needed to feel Cassie again after her interaction with her ex-husband. He knew it was a possessive thing, but he couldn't help it. JD was a man who was possessive about those he loved. "What did he want?"

Cassie shook her head. "Nothing really."

He knew better than that, but guessed she didn't want to discuss it with Gus and Nan. He'd find out later. Oh yes, he'd find out because no one made his Cassie frown as she had.

Cassie squeezed his hand and turned to the others. "What are you discussing?"

JD let the meeting with McKay go—for now—and focused on their case. "Well, we'll speak with the beta readers while Gus and Nan speak with the agent and editor."

Watching Cassie close her eyes and sigh made his gut clench. Something was terribly wrong.

"We can't interfere in the investigation, or Mike will have us arrested," she said.

Oh hell no. That asshole won't tell me what to do. "It won't be the first time we interfered." JD grinned. "And I'm sure it won't be the last."

"What's wrong, child?" Nan asked Cassie. "What did that man tell you to have you so tied up in knots like you are?"

Leave it to Nan to get to the point. JD loved the woman dearly. She'd always been like a mother to him when he needed it the most, even though most of the time he'd been a grown man when she'd helped him out as only a maternal figure would.

Turning all his attention to Cassie, JD raised his eyebrows. "Yeah, what did he say?" They'd talked for four minutes. Out of curiosity, he'd timed them. One could say a lot in four minutes. It didn't seem so, but an average person spoke 100-130 words a minute. Four hundred words were an awful lot for someone only to say if they only told the group to stay out of the case.

Cassie shrugged and stretched her neck in a circle as if needing to relax. She probably did after speaking with McKay.

Finally, she spilled the beans, "Nothing important. Except for us to stay out of the case. He didn't care that Missy hired us to prove her innocence. He wants us out of the way."

"Which means," JD said, "they want her for the crime if they don't want her to build a defense." His nostrils flared with his anger. As a former police detective, he had worked with the FBI before, and it never went well. JD always believed they decided their target and did whatever it took to prove it. And, sometimes, it seemed, they had a target and tried to find a crime. JD knew not all agents were that unethical, but his experience had certainly hardened him against the group.

Once, he had thought about going from police detective to FBI special agent. Then, he'd worked with a few agents. He hated the agency, especially since he now knew that Mike McKay worked there.

"We still help," Gus said with a nod of affirmation.

It was Gus and Nan's business, so if they wanted to

go up against the mighty FBI, he wouldn't argue. JD would do whatever the two asked of him. Anything, even if it was illegal. Well, he did have his limits.

Reminding himself that the FBI had been stupid in passing Cassie over for a field agent, he smiled at how she'd proven herself as a tough investigator with CI. The FBI's loss and his gain. In more ways than one. Oh, how JD loved the woman.

Could JD lose Cassie to her ex-husband? No, the two had ended badly. Yet, JD was worried. What if Cassie decided things were better with her ex-husband? What if McKay had come to tell her the bureau would take her back? Would Cassie go?

Too many questions and no answers. All he knew was that he needed to do something to prove that he loved her with all he had and that she was his. Flowers, wine and all that stuff must be in her future. He'd been slacking in the romantic department. It was time to step up and ensure she knew they were a forever couple. Maybe, just maybe, it was time to shop for that ring after all.

Chapter Eleven

The following morning, trouble was still on Cassie's mind. Why the heck did Mike, of all people, have to be the FBI special agent-in-charge of this investigation? Cassie's ire rose at the thought of it. Hadn't he wrecked her life enough? Snippets of yesterday's conversation returned to her mind.

"Cassie dear," he'd said to her, *"I know I screwed up. I'm sorry. I want a second chance."*

Like hell, she'd thought. But she hadn't known what to say or how to say it because she feared his backlash. So, she'd just mumbled that she was in a relationship.

"To that loser?" he'd questioned, nodding to JD.

That had made her back stiffen and her courage return. She would not let him cow her again. She'd endured enough beating down of her spirit thanks to Mike. She loved JD and nothing would change that. Not even a man she'd thought she'd loved before. *"What's it to you? We're through and there is no second chance."*

"I'll win you back. Now, about the case…."

Thinking of it again made Cassie's muscles tense. What would Mike try? Would he really attempt to destroy her and JD's relationship so she and Mike could be together again? She had so many unanswered questions that she shouldn't have since he had been her husband, but there they were. She had no idea what he would do now.

Had Mike been serious when he'd told her the FBI wanted her as a field agent? Finally? Cassie wasn't sure how she felt about that and didn't want to consider it at this point. But, oh, how she'd wanted to reach out and grab the opportunity. Would JD give up CI and move with Cassie to wherever she'd be stationed? Probably not. Actually, the idea of her leaving JD and CI was ludicrous.

"Good morning, Cassie," Nan said as Cassie entered the CI office.

"Morning, Nan." Cassie looked around for Gus. "Where's your other half?" She'd seldom seen the two apart. She smiled at the attachment the two elders shared.

Nan frowned, and her eyes held sadness. "He's got a stomach bug."

She could see Nan's worry, but what was she to say except, "Oh no. I hope he's better soon." Cassie took a seat behind her desk, feeling inadequate in this situation. There was no reason for her to be involved, and she had no idea what she could do to help.

The older woman nodded.

Before either could respond, the door opened, and JD walked in with one of his arms behind his back. Curiosity had one of Cassie's eyebrows rising. *Was he hurt?* was her first thought. However, his big smile told her he was up to something. JD brought his arm from behind his back and separated two bouquets with each hand. He handed one to Nan. "To my favorite lady." Then, he extended one beautiful bouquet of daisies to Cassie. "To the love of my life."

Cassie's heart melted on the spot. JD remembered from their childhood that her favorite flower was a daisy. Then, she wondered why he'd brought flowers. JD hadn't done that since she'd returned. Was he trying to butter her up for something?

Cassie eyed him but smiled. "Thank you, JD. These are perfect."

"Yes, thank you, JD," Nan said. "I'll get us a couple of vases." She disappeared in the back.

JD leaned down and kissed Cassie lightly on the lips. "I've missed you."

She ached for more of a kiss but knew he wouldn't give her one in the office. "What's the occasion?"

His eyes widened, and he touched his heart in mock hurt. "Why do I need an occasion to bring flowers to my two favorite women?"

Cassie knew something was up but left it alone. Then it hit her—Mike was in town. *Oh, JD. You've got nothing to worry about with him.*

JD gave her another quick kiss and stood. "What's the plan for today?"

Like he didn't know. JD set the plans every day for work. Cassie didn't mind since he knew more about being a PI than her. However, once she proved herself, Cassie would take the lead occasionally. "I thought we were headed to the first beta reader today." Thank goodness Missy had beta readers within a short drive. Had Missy planned it that way? According to her, she'd never met any of these readers face-to-face.

"Here's something with water," Nan said as she returned. She handed Cassie a blue mason jar that set off the white in the daisies.

"Where's Gus?" JD winked at Nan. "Has he finally

realized he's not good enough for you?"

Nan chuckled and playfully swatted JD's bicep. "You're incorrigible. He's just got an upset stomach."

JD drew in his brows. "He's never missed a day since I've been here."

"Well," Nan said, "he has now. Off with you two. You have a lot of work to do while treading around the mighty FBI."

Cassie stood. "Bail us out of jail if we get into trouble?"

"Always, my dear."

Then she remembered when Gus had put up a large bail amount to get JD released from jail. Yes, Gus and Nan would help if Mike decided to play dirty.

"Let's get moving." JD reached out and slid his hand behind her back, softly propelling her forward. "We've got a drive."

The drive was only a little over two hours, but with the interview and the return trip, it would make for a long day.

Settled inside JD's truck, they left the small CI office. JD put his hand over hers. "What's going on in that brain of yours?"

Lots of things, but what to tell him? Not about Mike. That would surely bring tension into the cab. Not about her concerns for Gus because that could be nothing. "I was thinking about the case. These beta readers have been with Missy for years. I can't imagine one of them suddenly deciding to act out her books."

JD shook his head and shrugged. "People snap. Disturbed people read into things a way we can't imagine."

Cassie pondered that while they drove to

Louisiana.

Arriving in Baton Rouge, JD pulled his truck up to a small—and she meant small—wooden home that had seen better days. At least it had survived hurricane season last year. She wished the owner luck in the upcoming year.

JD put the truck in park and turned off the engine. "Okay, beta reader number one."

Nodding, Cassie opened her notebook and read, "Raymond Green. He's been with her for five years. Missy describes him as an old military veteran who reads to fill the gap from losing his wife—of thirty years—six years ago." She looked up at the residence with sadness. She couldn't imagine losing JD after that many years together. Mentally shaking her head, Cassie reminded herself that they would need thirty years to even worry about it. Right now, they were in the dating stage.

"Let's do this." JD opened his truck door and smoothly stepped out like he'd probably done many times as a police officer and then detective.

On the other hand, Cassie clumsily exited the truck, towing her too-large name-brand bag with her. She should purchase a smaller bag. But it was nice to have everything she needed at hand. Plus, this had been her first extravagant purchase after she'd been accepted into the FBI. She wanted to get her money's worth out of it.

Walking up the concrete steps, JD looked at Cassie and nodded when he saw her ready. He knocked on the door. They probably should have called first, but they didn't want to spook their suspect if it happened to be one of those three. But in Cassie's mind, it had to be one of these three. Unless they had shared the manuscript. *Oh, please don't let that have happened. I like having just a few suspects.*

A gray-haired man, with a military cut, in a worn Saints T-shirt and jeans swung open the door. He eyed JD and Cassie, his gaze returning to JD. "I already told the other FBI agents all about my reading the book."

The other FBI agents. *Dang it*. She and JD shouldn't have waited overnight. Mike hadn't.

Cassie and JD looked at each other, then JD turned back to the man. "Raymond Green, I take it. We're not the FBI. We're here on Missy's behalf."

Raymond's face brightened. "Why didn't you say so." He opened the door wide. "Come on in." He saw Cassie look at the house with concern. "Don't worry. It's bigger inside than it appears."

Feeling guilty for showing her thoughts, Cassie entered behind JD. Raymond had been right; the place did appear larger inside.

He led them to a small living room, where they sat on a plastic-covered couch. Oh, how Cassie hated that.

"Sorry," Raymond said. "My Betty covered those when we first got them, and I don't have the heart to remove the plastic even though I despise the stuff."

As they sat, Cassie's heart bled for the man—thirty years and then being alone with all the memories in the home.

"I've wanted to sell this place and move to something that can withstand a storm, but, like the plastic on the furniture, I can't bear to part with the only home Betty and I had."

She and JD looked at each other, and Cassie saw the sadness in his eyes, with a longing that had nothing to do with sex. Maybe he longed for them to have that kind of relationship that lasted thirty years. Well, so did she. Only now wasn't the time to ponder that topic. They needed to focus on the case.

"My name is JD Walker, and this is Cassie McKay. We're with Coastal Investigation out of Gulf Islands, over in Mississippi. Missy hired us to help clear her name."

Cassie was glad he hadn't said "to find the real killer," as that would put off their suspects.

"As you've guessed, my name is Raymond Green. Raymond Abraham Green, and I want to help Missy in any way I can."

"Mr. Green," Cassie said, "it's nice to meet you. I'm a long-time friend of Missy's. I know what you do for her is important, and I appreciate the time and effort you put into helping her make her books special."

The older man blushed. No way he could be their killer. A man who blushes at a compliment couldn't turn around and harm a person. Or, could they?

"It's fun, actually." Raymond shifted, and the plastic underneath him creaked. "I never knew a position like this existed. I've always read thrillers and had my personal thoughts, but to give them along the way through a story. It's exhilarating."

It was also a zero-pay gig. Cassie had learned that beta readers were critical, but they were generally not paid. The author would gift them a signed copy of the book, dedicate a book to them, or give them gifts over the holidays. Each author was different. Missy didn't pay them, but she spoiled them in other ways with gifts, and she'd dedicated books to them.

JD cleared his throat. "How did you learn about

Missy's position of a beta reader?"

"I've been a reader of hers since her first book came out. I think she's the best. I love her writing. Anyhow, I read her newsletters, and in one of them, she asked for beta readers. Once I learned what they were, I applied. Missy made us take part in reading a manuscript and give our feedback to see how thorough we would be in the role." Raymond smiled. "I enjoyed the mission, tearing the manuscript apart. I only wish she'd write faster."

Mission? Oh, right, a military man. You can take the man out of the military, but you can't take the military out of the man. Or so Cassie had heard.

JD jumped right to their questioning. No, interrogation. "Tell us about the FBI visit." It'd been like JD had read her mind on that open-ended statement. Cassie wanted to know what Mike was doing. She didn't trust him. Maybe it was because he was her ex-husband, or because he wanted Missy for the crimes. Either way, Cassie knew trouble was brewing.

Raymond leaned forward in his seat and placed his forearms on his thighs, clasping his hands together. "They don't like Missy. That was for sure. I don't know how they think someone so sweet could do something so vile."

"What did they ask?" Cassie questioned.

Raymond looked at each of them. "Probably the same things you're going to ask."

Cassie highly doubted that. Yes, some questions would be the same, but she and JD were attempting to clear Missy, while Mike and his crew were trying to pin the murders on her.

"Humor us," JD said. "Remember, we're here to clear Missy. We need to know what the FBI said for us to know where to level our investigation."

Raymond nodded. "Makes sense. Well, firstly, I wouldn't say I liked the one in charge. Mike or something other. He has a hard-on for my Missy as the murderer."

Chapter Twelve

On the return drive, JD thought of how he would secure his beautiful Cassie's love, while she talked about the case. He couldn't blame her. It was her best friend. And, it should be foremost on JD's mind, but he didn't want to lose Cassie to her old life. What if Mike told her the FBI wanted to give her a chance as an agent? Would she leave him and go? It had been Cassie's life's dream. JD couldn't bear losing her a second time.

"I liked Raymond, but he did seem a bit possessive about Missy."

"What? Who?" he asked.

Cassie turned to him. "Where is your mind?"

Reaching over, his hand clasped hers on her thigh. "On you. Always on you."

She squeezed his hand. "I love you, too, but get your mind on this case. Please."

Hearing Cassie say she loved him helped stray his thoughts from the potential of losing her to Mike and her old life. "I liked the old geezer too. I don't think he's our guy."

"What about that possessiveness?" she asked.

JD thought a moment. The man had seemed as if Missy had been his good friend even though JD knew better. Missy kept it at author-reader, like employer-employee. While she was more friendly than an employer, she'd never made friends with her beta readers. Missy had assured him and Cassie that it wasn't because they weren't good people, it had just been a lack of time.

"Maybe he's read more into things. He does hear from Missy several times a week with chapters to read. Even though they're not personal messages, it might be all he gets, considering he's alone now." Would JD still live in the past if he lost Cassie before himself? It would crush him. JD would need to go forward for Henry Kyle and any children he and Cassie had.

That sparked a new thought. *Children.* Did he want more children? Did she want children? It was a challenging topic to broach since marriage still hadn't been put on the table.

"It's sad the way he still lives with things the way she wanted them, not the way he did," Cassie said.

JD could believe it. He wouldn't want to lose anything of Cassie and her memories. "His only cling to life right now is being Missy's beta reader. I don't think he'd want to lose it by acting out her scenes. Besides, he doesn't seem in shape enough to do the deeds. Plus, did you see his hands?"

"That was my thought also. They looked like he had arthritis in spades. It must pain him to type back the responses to Missy."

JD pulled in his brow in thought. "Maybe he uses speech-to-text software. We didn't ask."

"I know," Cassie said. "I didn't want to be so uncouth."

"Uncouth?" JD glanced at her with a wide grin, squeezing her hand. "Look at the South coming back out in you."

Cassie laughed. "It's true. My mom and everyone have started rubbing off on me. I found myself calling a kid screaming as having a hissy fit. And Mom caught me using y'all." She shook her head. "I was born in the South, and the South was never out of me."

JD turned briefly to her. Cassie was so lovely. He could barely believe they were back together. "If I have anything to say about it, you'll never leave the South again."

She stopped laughing.

Oh no, had he said the wrong thing? JD never meant to frighten her with his visions for them in the future, but sometimes his mouth acted without a filter. "I've got an idea," he said, trying to salvage the moment. "Since it's getting late, what if we have dinner? Just you and me."

"What about Henry Kyle?"

JD loved that she always put his son first, but tonight it would be the two of them. "If your mom can't watch him, we'll go tomorrow night."

Cassie released his hand, and he dropped it on her thigh, giving it a light squeeze. "I'll call Mom." She reached for her purse on the truck floorboard and extracted her cell.

After a quick call, Cassie assured him Patricia would watch his son longer than planned. Now, where to take her that would be romantic on such short notice? He doubted they could get into The Rack House and Spirits Steakhouse or The Chimneys without notice, but he bet they could get into Mary Mahoney's Old French House in Biloxi. His heart leaped at the thought. That was where he'd taken her for his senior prom. At the time, his friends helped him with a tux and transportation. He'd snuck out of the house so his old man wouldn't realize he was going to have fun. And, it had been fun and romantic.

"How about Mary Mahoney's?" he suggested.

"Am I dressed okay for there?"

He glanced at her, drinking in the sight of her as if he hadn't seen her for days. She wore navy slacks and a nice dressy blouse that complimented her perfectly. "You look beautiful."

"I didn't ask you that. But thank you."

"We're dressed okay," he assured her. Heck, he'd worn khakis and a polo, not his customary cargo pants and T-shirt, so he felt dressed up for any occasion.

Cassie's phone rang, and she checked the caller screen. She tensed and answered with his curiosity ablaze.

"Hello, Mike," she said, and JD's hackles rose.

"Yes, we did meet with Raymond Green."

She paused and listened to whatever garbage the asshole spewed.

"No, I'm on my way to dinner."

After a brief pause, she responded, "Not that it matters, but Mary Mahoney's. We can meet tomorrow instead."

She pulled her phone down and looked at it. "He hung up on me."

Another reason for JD to wipe that usual glum smirk off the man's face. "What did he want?"

"He was upset we interviewed Raymond Green. He said he needed to speak with me. I told him we could do it tomorrow."

Great. JD had something to look forward to about as much as a dentist's drill without Novocain. "Well, we'll put him aside until tomorrow."

Cassie grasped his hand from her thigh and tightened her small one around his. "That sounds like an excellent idea."

After a few quiet moments, Cassie said, "You know. I've only been to Mary Mahoney's with you. I've not been there otherwise."

JD thought for a moment. "Makes sense. You left before your senior year of high school and never returned until now." Boy, was he glad she'd come home. He squeezed her hand tightly.

As they drove Highway 90 toward their dinner location, Cassie looked out the passenger window. "It's hard to believe this beach is manmade. I mean, it doesn't look as pretty as the ones in Florida, but it still had to be a huge undertaking."

JD had never considered the birth of their beach and honestly couldn't care so long as it was there now for him and Henry Kyle to enjoy. His son loved to sail as much as he did. Of course, they'd had their little problems—parent versus stubborn child—but JD's life would never be complete without Henry Kyle in it. And Cassie.

They arrived at the restaurant and were escorted to a small table for two against a brick wall. There was a brief indecision over who would sit in the chair that provided a view of the front door. Ultimately, JD wanted the night to go well, so pleasing Cassie was more important than watching the door. At least she'd learned the importance of always knowing her surroundings.

JD sat, uncomfortable that his back was to the door but happy to see Cassie smiling. When the server approached behind him, he nearly jumped out of the chair. *Please Cassie*, he reminded himself. She wanted the front door view, and he let her have it. He had to learn that he couldn't always be in charge.

Without even a glance at the menu, Cassie ordered. "Fried crab claws for an appetizer."

JD agreed with that selection, although he remembered Cassie eating most of the crab claws last time, filling herself before dinner arrived.

They sent the male server away to get their beverages and order the appetizer. This hadn't been the romantic evening JD needed for Cassie. For that, he required flowers, candlelight, and privacy. Maybe he should cook for her and serve her at his home or on the boat. Yeah, on the boat. They would have privacy there. Plus, they hadn't christened the sailboat yet. JD hid his grin behind his menu. He didn't want to explain that thought—yet.

"Everything looks so good," Cassie said, peeking over the menu at him.

"Yes, it does." With his menu back on the table, JD's eyes were on Cassie alone.

She blushed. Yes, blushed at the compliment. He loved she still had a bit of innocence in her spirit.

JD picked up the menu again, knowing he would get the porterhouse with more than enough to bring home to his son. Heck, they needed a dog. He mentally shook his head at the diversion his thoughts took.

"I'm going to get the Shrimp and Lump Crabmeat Melba." Cassie nodded and placed her menu on the tiny table.

Chuckling, JD said, "I should have known if it had lump crabmeat in it, you'd have it."

She shrugged. "What can I say? I love crabmeat. What are you getting?"

JD placed the menu on the table. "Porterhouse."

Her eyes widened. "That's what you got last time. Why not try something different?"

He loved that she'd remembered his order from so long ago. "Because you don't mess with perfection."

Bill, the server, returned with JD's sweet tea and Cassie's glass of Chardonnay. They dictated their orders and Bill vanished.

With longing in his gaze, JD reached across the table and clasped one of Cassie's hands in his. "I had a great day with you." Okay, not the best line to begin a conversation. He had to do better than that tonight.

Cassie beamed at him, and his stomach flipped in excitement. "I did too. It was a great trip back and forth to Louisiana. I enjoyed seeing old sights along the way."

"Do you like dogs?" he blurted out. What the hell was wrong with him? It was like he couldn't speak around Cassie. Good grief, JD loved this woman and had never been this nervous before. Okay, maybe when they'd first made love, but other than that, this took the cake.

Bill appeared and placed their appetizer on the table, then vanished without a word. The guy could have been a spook with his stealth.

Cassie's eyes widened at the pile of fried crab claws. She grabbed one and nodded. "Yes, I like dogs. Why do you ask?"

JD shrugged and watched her put the crab claw in her mouth and slowly remove it, sans the crabmeat. He shifted in his seat to get more comfortable as his need for her became evident. "I think Henry Kyle needs a dog."

"That's a great idea." Cassie dropped the cleaned claw on the plate and grasped another fried claw. "Any particular breed?"

JD grabbed a crab claw and waved it while he spoke. "Whatever the shelter has to offer."

Another crab claw down for Cassie. "Are you going to let Henry Kyle pick the dog or are you going to pick one for him?"

They paused while Bill served their entrees. "Anything else?" the waiter asked.

Shaking her head, Cassie said, "No" simultaneously as JD.

Continuing the conversation before the interruptions, JD said, "I thought—" He broke off at Cassie's sudden wide eyes and O on her lips.

"Hello, Cassie," McKay said from behind JD.

Chapter Thirteen

Cassie froze at the sight of her ex-husband. What was Mike doing at the restaurant? Why couldn't he just leave her alone? She didn't know the answers to those questions, but Cassie planned to find out or give him a good smack to the jaw. Okay, she wouldn't resort to violence, but in dreams....

"Wh-What are you doing here?" she struggled to ask.

JD stood and turned to Mike. "Yeah, what the hell are you doing here?"

It was her fault. She'd told him where they were going. She hadn't meant it as an invitation. Now she had two alphas staring each other down.

Bill, bless him, appeared. "Is there a problem?" he asked quietly.

JD said, "Yes, he wasn't invited to dinner."

The waiter looked at her, and she nodded in agreement. Bill turned back to Mike. "Sir, I'm going to have to ask you to put your name on the waitlist and stay out front or leave."

Mike gave his "I'm all that and a bucket of chicken" grin, and she knew what would come next. Yep, he flashed his badge like that was a golden pass. "I'm FBI."

Bill stood stoically, as if he saw a badge every day. "Good for you."

Cassie almost burst out laughing. No one had ever down-played Mike's FBI badge before.

"Now," Bill continued, "unless you plan to arrest these two, please go out front or leave."

Cassie wanted to stand up and cheer for the waiter. She imagined JD just jumped the man's tip to nearly fifty percent or more.

"They're wanted for questioning," Mike said to Bill.

"No, we're not," JD said. "This is his ex-wife, and he's trying to make trouble."

Bill's eyebrows rose. "Gentlemen, I will not have a scene in here. So, take this outside or you"—Bill pointed to Mike— "leave."

"All right," Mike said. "Bring them some to-go boxes and the bill. Then, we'll leave."

Once again, Bill glanced at Cassie as if she was the only sane one at the table. She slightly nodded, and Bill spun on his heels, striding away.

"I'll wait for you outside," Mike said as he turned and walked away.

JD stared after him, waiting until Mike exited before he sat. "What an asshole." He placed his napkin back in his lap and picked up his fork.

As he dug into his fare, Cassie asked, "Aren't we leaving to meet with him?"

With his fork midway to his mouth, JD stopped and narrowed his eyes at her. "Is that what you want to do?"

Nervously, she shook her head. "No." She didn't want a fight between the two men.

JD nodded. "Then eat. We're not leaving for that putz."

Bill returned with to-go boxes and the bill. "Good, he left. Are you two staying, or do you want these boxes?"

Smiling, JD said, "We're staying."

Nodding, Bill turned and left the table with the empty to-go boxes.

Trying to keep the nervousness out of her voice, Cassie asked, "Can't he arrest us or something for not going to meet him?"

JD raised an eyebrow. "For what? No, Cassie. And if he tries, I'll have his badge."

Cassie must have looked doubtful because JD reached across and took her hand. "Honey, we've done nothing wrong. There's nothing he can arrest us for. Now," —he dropped her hand and reached for his knife— "eat."

How could she eat when Mike had ruined her appetite? The lump crabmeat looked so good, yet Cassie couldn't take a bite.

Seeing her distress, JD dropped his fork and knife. "Cassie, please, don't let that ass ruin our evening." Again, he reached across the table for her hand, intertwining his fingers with hers. "Listen, we have this time without work or family. It's just you and me. Let's enjoy the meal."

"I just worry," she said, loving his thumb caressing her palm.

"I know you do, and that's one of the things I love about you. You care. But McKay can't do a thing to us unless he manufactures something."

"But we talked to a potential suspect today."

JD shrugged. "So. There's no law against it. We're not interfering, no matter what he says. We're just asking questions to assist our client."

Cassie sighed. "I've just not had a case when we've gone against the FBI before."

"I know. It's okay. I won't get us arrested. At least," —he wickedly grinned— "not both of us."

Laughing, she shook her head. "You're something else."

"I know." His grin broadened. "That's why you love me so much."

She couldn't help the nod. "Yes, I do."

"I love you, too." He dropped her hand and pointed to her plate. "Now, eat."

Still unsure, but taking JD's direction, Cassie took a bite and smiled. The food tasted fabulous. After two bites, she'd forgotten all about Mike. She focused on the man in front of her, the meal, and the romantic atmosphere. Romantic. Had that been JD's intent for tonight? Cassie wondered why since JD had done nothing romantic since they'd first come back together months ago—except the flowers.

They went back to discussing the dog as if the conversation had not been interrupted.

"Anyhow," JD said, "Whatever the pound has is fine with me, and I'm sure it will be with Henry Kyle."

"Are you going to surprise him, or are you going to take him with you?" she asked again.

"I had thought to surprise him, but now I think I want him to select. Maybe he'll feel a bond with one, no matter the age or breed."

After their meal, Cassie noticed Bill blocking Mike from entering the restaurant area from the front. "Uh oh," she said, "he's back and looking more pissed than before."

JD didn't even glance around. "Do you want dessert?" he asked, like she hadn't just said an FBI agent was raging about them.

Cassie patted her belly. "I couldn't take another bite."

Bill came back to the table. "How was everything?" He took their nearly empty plates. "Did you want dessert?"

She almost laughed at how both men were willingly blowing off Mike. She'd seen her ex-husband throw his weight around and didn't want to be part of his failure to be in charge.

"We're good," JD said. "Just the check, please."

Cassie reached for her purse.

"I've got it," JD said.

"I just wanted to add to the tip. Bill was excellent at handling Mike."

"Don't worry. I'm giving him a hundred dollars."

She gulped. The waiter deserved it, but that made for an expensive night they barely got to enjoy. Unless you factor in the Mike entertainment.

After signing the check and closing the book, JD smiled, and his heated gaze drove her libido crazy.

"Are you ready?"

"For?" she asked breathlessly, unable to break eye contact. For an instant, she'd forgotten about Mike and everything else. Cassie could drown in those sexy eyes of his.

"Our future."

Oh no. Was JD going to propose? Here? Now? Nervously, she said, "Sure, but Mike's waiting."

His nostrils flared, and anger flashed briefly in his gaze before it softened. "You're right. Let's get this show on the road." He stood and offered her a hand to do likewise. Before they parted, JD placed a brief kiss on her lips. "I love you, Cassie."

"I love you, too," she whispered.

Clasping her hand, he turned. "Let's do this."

They waved bye to Bill and proceeded to the exit and the angry FBI agent beyond.

Outside the restaurant, Mike paced in front of a metal bench. When he noticed them, he stopped and whirled. "I should have you two arrested for ignoring my summons."

JD squeezed her hand, and it gave her strength.

"For what?" JD asked. "I didn't see an official summons." He turned to Cassie. "Did you, sweetheart?"

Was he trying to rile Mike? She'd seen Mike's temper and didn't want any part of it, but JD seemed to have the advantage in this conversation. Cassie shook her head. "I didn't see anything official."

Face red, hands fisted, Mike growled, "The badge is official enough."

"Look, McKay, I'm on a date with the love of my life, and you are really putting a damper on the romance. Would you get to the point? What the hell are you doing here?"

When Mike's eyes bulged and his jaw visibly clicked, Cassie worried he'd have an aneurysm. She'd never seen him this hot-tempered.

"You two are interfering, and I told you I wouldn't have it." Mike's annoyance bled into his tone.

JD shrugged. "We just talked to an employee of our client. Nothing else. Are you saying we can't speak to her employees? That would be restrictive to our business, plus, I'm certain you can't put that stipulation on us."

Cassie almost gasped at JD's response. She wondered if these two men were going to come to blows.

"Cassie," Mike said, "talk some sense into this prick. You don't want me to arrest him."

Not wanting to be pulled into their power struggle, she shrugged. "I don't control him." And to show Mike her loyalty to JD, she reached up and kissed him on the cheek. "Can we go home?" They didn't have a home together, but Mike might not know that yet. Then again, she was sure Mike knew everything since he'd come to town. Probably even before. Undoubtedly, he asked for this assignment just to get back at her. His desire to get back together had to be bull crap. He hated to lose, was all.

JD didn't move a muscle when she kissed him, nor did he break eye contact with Mike. "Yes, love, we can."

Mike sputtered as they walked around him. "Keep interfering, and I'll have you arrested."

"Keep moving," JD whispered to her. "Don't let him know his ranting bothers you."

"Cassie, you're on the wrong side here. Be careful," Mike yelled.

Oh, definitely no. She'd been on the wrong side before. After seeing the FBI railroad Missy, Cassie knew CI was right for her. She glanced at JD. She'd been stupid and desperate with Mike. With JD, her heart filled with love and affection, like it was meant to be.

Opening her door, JD leaned down and whispered in her ear, "I love you."

Cassie turned and threw her arms around him and kissed him deep, tongues and all. Screw Mike McKay. She hoped he got a good view of the love that flowed between her and JD. Because Mike could go to hell. She was going to participate in helping Missy, and she wouldn't fall for Mike's tricks to attempt to win her back.

After breaking the kiss, she gazed into JD's eyes. "I love you, too."

"Good." Grinning, he swatted her behind. "Get in the truck, beautiful. It's time for me to take you home."

She agreed but wondered which home he meant. Hers with all the family, or his with no one to interrupt them?

On his way to his side of the truck, she noticed he used his phone for a call. Getting into the vehicle, he said, "Thanks, Patricia," before ending the conversation.

"How is Henry Kyle?" Cassie asked as JD buckled his seat belt.

JD started the truck and turned to her, heat burning in his gaze. "He's fine and staying the night with Patricia. All night."

Chapter Fourteen

JD smiled at the beautiful woman sleeping in his arms. He needed to wake her soon and take her home. She'd want to shower and change before work. He wouldn't shame her by making her show up at work in the same clothes as the day prior. Although, that might shut up the fat-mouthed McKay for a while.

He wanted her to feel comfortable telling him what McKay had said to her at CI the other day. She remained silent regarding that conversation, and it irked him. JD didn't know how to broach the subject without putting Cassie's back up.

Cassie moved in his arms, and a small sigh escaped her lips. JD had never seen a sexier woman—with or without clothing. Now, however, was not the time to get aroused. They needed to get moving.

"Cassie," he whispered. "It's time to wake up, honey."

"Hmm," she responded, still asleep.

JD kissed her lips. Then he kissed her top lip, bottom lip, and exposed cheek, then kissed a path down the silky skin on her neck.

Cassie moaned and arched her neck. "I love you waking me this way."

He leaned away, getting out of her path, knowing what would transpire next.

She bolted up in bed, the sheet falling below her

luscious breasts. "Oh my God, it's morning. We slept in! I've got to get home."

Chuckling, JD put his hands behind his head and watched as she jumped from bed, searching for her clothing.

"Hurry," she said. "We've got to go."

Not in the "hurry" *she* wanted, JD admired her sleek body as she stepped into her clothing. He knew they needed to get a move on, but he liked the show.

"JD," she said in a demanding voice. "Get up."

Not wanting to get Cassie riled, JD tossed the sheet off and stepped from the bed. After pulling on briefs and his cargo shorts, he grabbed her arms, stalling her from putting her shirt on, and kissed her. "Settle down. Your mom doesn't give you a curfew."

"I know. But Henry Kyle. What must he think?"

Having her worry about his son warmed his heart more than he could have expected. JD wanted to kick himself for not thinking of his son's feelings first, though. That should have been his primary thought process, not how much he wanted Cassie in his bed, though conflicted about why he couldn't have both thoughts.

"He'll be fine. He's not a kid," JD reminded her. Now, though, he wondered what his son thought of Cassie staying overnight at their home. He and Cassie had time together before, but not an entire night. At least, he had forethought to have his son stay overnight away with Pat. On reflection, since Cassie didn't come home last night, and he'd bring her home this morning, he wouldn't be able to fool Henry Kyle as to what occurred.

Seeing her point in the matter, he dropped his arms

and stepped back. "Let's grab breakfast on the way home. We'll pick up donuts." He grinned. "No one gets upset when you bring them hot donuts."

JD laughed when Cassie rolled her eyes. Swatting her lightly on the bottom, they left for the trek to the donut shop.

On the drive to Cassie's home, JD downed two of the warm donuts, licking the tasty glaze from his fingers.

"You're worse than a kid unable to wait until you get home to eat," Cassie jested.

"They're best hot." She was lucky he hadn't grabbed one right off the conveyor belt after it received the glaze.

When they arrived at Cassie's home, she sat in the truck momentarily. "What are we going to tell them?"

JD laughed again. This woman warmed his heart. "What do you mean?"

She turned, her face flaming red in embarrassment. "About last night?"

"Cassie, honey, we're adults. There is nothing we need to say," he assured her.

After a moment, she nodded. "You're right, of course."

They exited the truck and entered the house. "Donuts," he said.

Cassie said, "Only ten since JD sucked down two on the drive."

Over coffee, and OJ for Henry Kyle, they talked about the upcoming day. Patricia and Henry Kyle were taking a field trip to the Maritime and Seafood Industry Museum to enhance his learning. JD and Cassie were, of course, going to work.

Before leaving, JD pulled Henry Kyle aside. "How are you, champ?"

"Good, Dad."

"Are you okay with last night?"

Henry Kyle looked confused, then as if a lightbulb turned on, he said, "You mean you and Miss Cassie staying together?"

Warily, JD nodded. "Yes, that."

Shrugging, Henry Kyle looked away. "I'm fine with it."

JD wasn't one hundred percent certain his son was fine with it, but now wasn't the time to dive into his feelings on the matter. That would be for the evening they would spend together.

"Have fun today."

"Thanks, Dad." The boy zoomed off to grab another donut.

Shaking his head, JD wondered about that bottomless pit his son had for a stomach. Catching Cassie's gaze, he nodded toward the door to let her know it was time to leave. Since they'd left her Jeep at CI the day prior, they'd have to ride in together. Nothing like flaunting their evening to everyone. He was sure she wouldn't feel comfortable with everyone knowing she had slept over, even though they were adults.

Cassie kissed her mom's cheek. "I'll see you tonight, Mom."

Patricia smiled. "Okay, darling. Have a good day."

"We will."

JD loved how she included him, even though Patricia hadn't mentioned "we."

On the way to his truck, Cassie's phone rang. If it

was that damn Mike again, JD might have to go old-fashioned and call him out.

Cassie stopped and answered the call. "Hi, Missy."

JD halted after seeing the concerned look on Cassie's face.

"I hate to say it, but you must call the FBI."

JD's hackles rose. Something was wrong in Missy's world. Well, besides being considered a potential murderer.

"Don't touch it. Would you take a picture of it for us?"

Watching Cassie nod, JD wanted to grab the phone and put it on speaker. Don't touch what?

"All right. We'll see you after the FBI leaves you." She ended the call and looked at him. "Missy just received a letter from a fan. One who said he was killing for her."

Well, the day got a lot more interesting.

Chapter Fifteen

Cassie pulled up Missy's message on her phone and opened the photo. She read the letter out loud to JD.

"Ardent Fan? Read between the lines? What kind of crackpot is this?" he asked.

"I don't know," Cassie replied, "but it is unnerving."

"Let's table this until we get to the office. Gus and Nan need to see this, plus I'd like a printed copy before McKay confiscates your phone. He'll probably ask Missy if she took a picture, and she'll tell him she sent you a copy of the letter."

Cassie sighed. "She would because she's honest and forthright." This should help the FBI take their eye off Missy now. Or at least she hoped it would. They might think Missy sent it to get the focus off herself. Anything was possible with Mike and the FBI.

Arriving at the CI office, they hustled inside to print the letter and have it in their hands. Cassie noticed Gus and Nan missing. She turned to Daisy. "Where are Gus and Nan?"

"Nan made Gus go to the doctor for his stomachache."

Worried it might be more severe than Nan had let on, Cassie wanted to call her but knew if they were in the doctor's office, she wouldn't answer. At least, Gus and Nan had spoken with the editor and agent before Gus's stomach bug warranted a medical appointment.

"Gus went to the doctor?" JD looked stunned.

Daisy nodded. "I know, right? Nan insisted, though."

JD shook his head. "That old geyser wouldn't go to the doctor if it wasn't serious. He thinks they're all bloodsucking quacks."

"We'll find out later," Daisy said.

Cassie, half-listening to JD and Daisy, connected to the office printer to print what would technically be evidence in a murder case. What would the penalty be for having this in her possession? She would delete it from her phone as soon as she printed it. Just in case Mike got a bug up his butt and decided to check. And, to aggravate both her and JD, Mike might.

Mike. Why must he arrive in her life now and attempt to ruin it? He showed up at the dinner and threatened to arrest them. Cassie had been frightened, but JD's confidence helped her straighten her back and be defiant in the end.

"Cassie?" JD asked.

She mentally shook her head and turned to him. "Yes?"

He searched her eyes. "Where were you?"

Crap. She needed to focus on this case, not the mess Mike might make in her life. With JD by her side, she would be fine.

Daisy handed her a copy of the letter, fresh from the printer. Wow, another nice thing the woman had done for her. She had heightened hopes for their work relationship, after all.

Reading over the letter again, Cassie sighed. What

a sicko. How could this person think Missy wanted him to kill people on her behalf? And the love thing bothered Cassie to no end.

"Well?" she asked the others.

Daisy's eyes widened as she read the letter for the first time. "Oh, my goodness."

JD shook his head. "We've got to help the FBI find this killer before he decides it's time to physically or actively begin this relationship with Missy."

Shaking her head, Cassie wondered out loud, "I will forever do your bidding." She dropped the paper on her desk and flopped into her chair. "This could make Missy stop writing."

"No!" Daisy screamed. Then she cleared her throat. Blushing, she said, "I mean, it would be a travesty if she stopped writing. She has many readers who are impacted by her stories."

"Yeah," JD said sarcastically. "Especially this one." He gestured to the paper in his hands.

Vehicles arrived, and Cassie stood. Missy and her entourage walked into the office. She wondered how weird it would be with two people always at your heels, even if one were your agent. Having a newspaper reporter with her most of the time would annoy Cassie like crazy. She'd constantly be minding her "P's" and "Q's."

"Good morning, Missy," Daisy said, standing at her desk with a bright smile.

"Good morning, Daisy. I forgot. Did you want me to sign your copy of my book?" Missy asked.

If nothing else came from this meeting, Daisy was happier and more satisfied than Cassie had ever seen her. It was time she got some due for the hard work she did, even if that due had nothing to do with the office.

"What a letter," Carl said gleefully.

Cassie wanted to slap him. Newspaper reporters were so morbid sometimes. They wanted a story at any cost, and this was a good one.

"You can't print this," JD stated. "If you do, McKay and the FBI will know Missy shared it, and she'd be in trouble."

Cassie's eyes widened. She hadn't thought of the trouble Missy would be in. She had, but not really putting anything specific on it—like impeding an FBI investigation and sharing evidence in the mix. Good grief. Could this get any more messed up?

"Okay," JD continued, keeping the meeting on target. "We've only spoken with one beta reader, and we're leaning on the assumption it is one of them since Robert and Missy's editor turned up clean."

Robert nodded like that had been a no-brainer. "Right, we didn't see the entire thing until it was finished."

So, that left it to a beta reader. *Unless it was pirated or shared.* Once again, Cassie hoped that wasn't the case.

"What can I do to help?" Missy asked.

Cassie had been such a terrible friend. She'd not made time to speak with Missy alone to see how she was doing. "Are you writing a new novel?"

Missy nodded. "I just finished the outline."

"Don't share it with anyone," JD directed.

"Not even me?" Robert asked, looking aghast at JD's statement.

"Not even you," JD stated.

Robert's brows furrowed, followed by a loud

"Hmph."

"What about me?" Carl asked with a smile.

"You're not part of this equation," Cassie said, slightly nastier than intended. If Carl got his hands on it, everyone would know Missy's story before she ever finished writing it. Dang reporters.

Another vehicle pulled up outside, and Cassie sighed. Finally, Gus and Nan. She had worried about Gus's health since Nan had forced him to go to the doctor.

Only it was Agents Angler and Miles.

Seeing them in the parking lot, everyone with a copy of the letter rushed to hide it. When the FBI agents walked in, the group looked innocent as a newborn.

Agent Angler scanned the room and nodded at everyone when he entered. His eyes rested on Missy. "Ma'am," he said to the author.

Gah, another besotted man. How many did poor Missy have following her around?

"What can we do for you, agents?" JD stood in front of the group around the table.

Agent Angler cleared his throat. "We know you have a copy of the letter."

No one moved or said a word.

"Right," the agent continued. "We're asking you, Carl, not to print this. It's evidence, and we must keep it back from the public forum for now."

Carl sighed and muttered under his breath. "Sure thing."

That made Cassie wonder if the reporter had planned to share at least snippets in his upcoming article. The series about Missy had two of five pieces printed to date.

Agent Angler looked uncomfortable, pulling on his tie and tucking it into his jacket. "Well, then. We are reminding you all to stay out of our investigation."

JD said, "No."

Cassie almost laughed at the two agents' expressions. They obviously hadn't expected a pushback. JD was the only person she knew who fought the FBI. It was fun. Although not fun enough to go to jail over. She hoped JD knew when to draw the line.

"Well," Agent Angler said, "just stay out of our way." He nodded and exited with Agent Miles on his heels.

The group watched the agents in the parking lot until they entered their nondescript government vehicle.

"It's time we moved faster in finding this sicko," JD said.

Cassie couldn't agree more.

Chapter Sixteen

Before they left to meet with beta readers two and three, Cassie asked JD for time to sit with Missy. After glancing at her friend's worried expression, he agreed to a few minutes.

"Missy," Cassie said, drawing her attention from the group, "want to come with me to get the coffee going?" She didn't have an office and didn't want to intrude on Gus and Nan's office, so the break room it was.

"Sure." Missy's relieved look told Cassie she was on the right track.

As Cassie set up the coffee pot, Missy looked around the small room. "How do you like it here?"

Hearing the distraught in her friend's voice, Cassie decided to allow her to lead the conversation, and if it wasn't about Missy, so be it. "I love it." Cassie did, and not only because she worked with JD. They helped those accused of a crime find evidence to prove their innocence. Luckily, they hadn't a case of someone who turned out to be guilty, but Cassie had only been here for less than six months.

"I'm glad. I hate the FBI didn't see this side of you."

Cassie considered it. Did she want to be an FBI agent, or was it the overall investigation piece she wanted? She couldn't be like Mike or the two agents who had recently departed the office. "You know, I'm glad they didn't. I think this is a better fit for me." She gestured for Missy to sit at the small table with two chairs in the room. "Besides, I like wearing something other than suits every day."

Missy laughed and snorted. "You always hated that part of your old job." She put her face in her hands. "Oh, Cassie, this is so messed up."

Cassie placed a hand on Missy's shoulder, wishing she could give her friend a big hug. "I know, but you haven't done anything wrong."

"Of course I did. I picked those who read my book early. I created that plot and method of murder. It's all my fault."

"Oh, Missy." Cassie sighed. She guessed she would feel the same way, but how to help her friend? An idea formed. "Well then, help us."

Missy looked up with watery eyes and sniffed. "How exactly?"

"You can go back through all the notes and input from your beta readers on this novel and see if anything seems off—different from their previous input."

Brightening, Missy said, "I can do that. Is there anything specific I should look for?"

It wasn't like someone would say "I'm going to kill for you," in their feedback. "Just anything that seems different." She cocked her head and searched her friend's face. "How are you doing otherwise?"

"Robert won't leave me alone until this is resolved. I'm not his only client, so I hate that he's spending all his time chaperoning me and Carl." She laughed. "Well, not chaperoning in the way one would think. He's considering everything that Carl asks and writes down. I'm lucky he's so diligent because I can't focus on all this."

"How are the interviews coming along? Shouldn't Carl have enough to finish his series?"

"Yes," Missy said, pushing ebony hair behind her ear. "This FBI thing has him salivating, and he wants to stay around until it's resolved. Robert approved it as long as nothing was printed until it was over. Carl fought that but eventually agreed."

"Hmph," Cassie said. Too many people were in Missy's life right now when she needed her friend–the friend who hadn't been there for her until now.

"What can I do to help you deal with this? I imagine it's a tough case in one's life."

Missy smiled and patted Cassie's hand. "You show that I'm innocent so the FBI will leave me alone."

Cassie nodded. "I imagine this letter will do it." Who knew with the FBI?

"Besides..." Missy stood. "If it's someone close to me—even a beta reader—I want them out of my life, *period*, but definitely before resuming having anyone see my storyline before publication."

Cassie knew having someone read along the way helped Missy catch things early. "We'll find out who did it." She hoped she hadn't just assured Missy of something she couldn't deliver. But she and JD would give it their all. Thinking of all, Cassie also stood. "It's time we meet with your other two beta readers. Since they're both in the sticks in Louisiana, we hope to meet with them both today."

"You know, I knew my readers lived close, but I never imagined they lived that close to me." Missy shuddered. "A killer in the midst." Missy paused, a smile now gracing her face. "Hey, that's a good plot and book title."

Just like that, Cassie knew her friend would be all right. "Okay, let's get this show on the road."

They exited the break room, where Cassie felt she'd left her emotions, only to see Gus and Nan in the outer space with a solemn atmosphere. What had happened?

Turning to JD to see what had created this mood, he shook his head to forestall any comment from her. *Okay, not good.*

As if nothing serious was in the air, Robert asked, "What are you doing next? Do you feel Raymond isn't your guy?"

JD took a moment before he answered. "We didn't say he wasn't our guy. He just didn't strike us as a killer. That doesn't mean he isn't."

Robert nodded. "Oh."

Nan waved her hand to the group. "Continue what you were doing. We need to free Missy from the FBI as soon as possible. Don't count on the letter doing it. They will keep her as a person of interest. Now," —she looked at JD and Cassie— "do what you do."

They stood for a moment because Cassie wouldn't move until JD did. Something was going on.

"*Asteur, cher,*" Gus said. "I be fine."

Now. Gus wanted them out of the office. It must be bad.

JD nodded and reached for Cassie's hand. She grabbed her bag, and they left the office with Missy and her entourage in tow.

"Bye, Cassie," Missy said.

Cassie turned. "We'll talk later."

Missy nodded and smiled.

In the truck, JD sat there staring out the windshield.

"What?" she finally asked.

He turned to her. "Nan said it might be cancer."

Cassie quickly put her hand to her mouth, shocked. "No."

"Yeah." He started the truck and put it in reverse.

"Did she say it was or it might be?"

He looked her in the eyes. "Might be."

She nodded. "Good. That means it might not be. Doctors like to give the worst-case scenario upfront. They won't know this quickly if it was cancer. Let's pray it isn't." She and JD had never discussed religion, but she hoped he prayed, at least for his friend.

Once on the highway, JD asked, "Okay, give me the rundown on the other two beta readers. I want to knock them both out today."

Cassie opened the folder she'd kept with Missy's notes, including the letter from her "ardent fan." "Looks like we have Alex Finley and David Maynard. Both have been with Missy for three years. She added them when two others decided they didn't wish to be beta readers any longer." Cassie couldn't imagine not wanting to read a novel as it was written, especially one that surely would make the *NYT* charts.

After entering the addresses in the truck's GPS, Cassie said, "We can hit Alex in an hour and a half, so I think we should go to him first." Again, she hated not calling before showing up, but she understood JD's style since one might be a killer. Why prepare them to kill the two of them for interfering?

"Sounds good," JD said and put an arm on the back of the seat. "If it's not one of them, we're back to square one, and I don't know where else to look."

Neither did Cassie. Yet, she didn't expect the killer to say, "Here I am. Arrest me." Her first case with JD had been a murder case, where JD had been suspected and arrested, then later released. They still worked the case to find out the real killer's identity, since the victim had been Henry Kyle's mother.

JD remained silent most of the drive. Cassie guessed it was because he thought about Gus, not the case. She knew the man too well, along with his relationship with the older man. *Please don't let it be cancer.*

As they turned off the highway onto roads leading to Finley's home, Cassie opened her folder again, refreshing them on the person they were to interview. "This is Alex Finley. He's been with Missy for three years. He applied and was the strongest candidate she'd ever seen. From what he's shared with her, he's single—not sure if it means never married, divorced, or widowed—and lives alone."

Cassie closed the folder. *What was with these thriller beta readers?* They were single men who lived alone. How odd that they had earned spots on the team. If this had been a romance, she'd expected women. It would have been easier to find the murderer since they assumed the killer was male or very strong. Although, as Lucy had said, "People will surprise the hell out of you." Good grief, she hated quoting the woman. Thank goodness Lucy wasn't showing up at the office or bothering them. Of course, Cassie wasn't with JD all the time. The bitch could be calling him during those off-times.

Enough. She couldn't let her mind wander there.

Her uncertainty had to stop. JD loved her and only her. She had no doubts that he'd remain faithful to her. So, she had to put aside Lucy's desire to reunite with JD.

"Here we are." JD pulled into a dirt driveway.

Another shack of sorts. There were poor people in Louisiana, and many lived like this, but she hated it for them because a good hurricane would destroy their home.

"No vehicles," she stated the obvious.

JD put the truck in park but left it running. "Maybe we should have called." He gave her a cock-eyed grin that told her he thought her suggestion a good one, and one he shouldn't have ignored.

"Maybe we should have." Cassie smiled.

"Let's see if someone is home." JD turned the truck off and opened the driver's door.

Cassie exited also and met JD at the front of the vehicle. "It looks vacant." The lawn had not been given attention in a long time. There were a few cobwebs on the corners of the porch. It scared her to go into the house if this was how Alex kept his curb appeal, or rather *unappeal*.

They stepped onto the nice-sized porch, and JD rang the doorbell. In this rundown home, they had an electronic doorbell with a camera to observe them. Maybe the inside wouldn't be so bad.

After several doorbell rings and knocks, JD gave up. "We'll swing by on the way home. If he's not here, we'll call and schedule a time." He shook his head. "I just hate giving anyone time to prepare for us. It'd be different if they were witnesses. But one of them might be a murderer."

True. And, if Missy was correct, there was still one

more murder to occur before this story ended. Could they find the killer before another innocent was murdered?

Chapter Seventeen

Since neither beta reader had been home, JD and Cassie returned early. They'd try again tomorrow. He'd consider calling them first, but he still wanted that surprise factor right now. The surprise would be on him if they were never home when he arrived.

At a taco shop, JD watched Henry Kyle wolf down almost a dozen tacos and felt the heartburn the kid should have. But a kid's iron stomach and all....

"Thanks for the tacos, Dad." Henry Kyle took another bite.

Shaking his head, JD wondered if he would have to take a second job to keep his son fed. Did all kids eat that much? "You're welcome."

Sitting in the tiny shop, JD noticed only a few customers inside. Perfect. He wanted to speak with his son about two things; one needed some privacy. He thought of talking later, but his son was relaxed now.

JD cleared his throat. "I wanted to speak with you about something important."

"I know," Henry Kyle said, "you and Miss Cassie."

Damn him for having such a bright and perceptive son. "Yes. You know I love her."

"Yeah. You guys smooch all the time. It's kind of gross." He pulled another hard-shell taco from the wrapper and bit into it.

"I'd like to have her in our lives."

"She already is," Henry Kyle said. "We're almost always together when you're not at work."

Shaking his head, JD thought of what to say. "I want her in our lives, permanently."

Henry Kyle stopped with the half-eaten taco midway to his mouth. "You mean live with us?" he asked hesitantly.

Here goes. "I am thinking of asking her to be my wife."

His son stared away.

"How would you feel about her being in our lives that way?"

"You mean, like my mother and all?"

JD gulped down his nervousness. "Yes. Like that, but she wouldn't replace your mother. That would also make Miss Pat your grandmother."

Henry Kyle bit his lower lip, then sighed. "I don't know. I hadn't thought of her being my mother or having a grandmother. I mean, I like Miss Cassie and all, but I'm not sure I want another mother."

JD's heart sank to the bottom of his stomach. He needed Henry Kyle on board, or things would be a battle in the household, and he didn't want that, nor would Cassie. "Will you think about it? I really want her in our lives as my wife." *And your mother*, he wanted to add, but knew those words didn't need to be repeated.

"Sure, Dad." His son returned to eating, not realizing he'd just put a huge hole in his father's world.

"I have something else to speak with you about."

"Okay," his son said with his mouth full of food.

"Gross."

After swallowing, Henry Kyle said, "Sorry, Dad."

"What do you think about getting a dog? We have a fenced yard and room in the house for one."

His son's eyes brightened. "For real, Dad?"

"Yes, champ, for real."

"Can we get one right now?" Henry Kyle bounced in his seat, ready to bolt from the shop to get a dog.

JD looked at his watch. "We might make it in time. Just know they're closing soon, so we can't take long. If you don't like one, or can't pick, we'll have to return tomorrow."

"Okay."

After cleaning their trash, they hurried to the truck and the Gulf Islands Humane Society. They were, thankfully, a no-kill shelter, which meant they were probably busting at the seams with animals. Surely his son would find one that he loved.

Was JD trying too hard as a father? Was he going too fast? They'd just bought a home and had barely settled into it. But he remembered wanting a dog when he was a boy; his father wouldn't allow it, which was probably a good thing because he wouldn't have trusted his father not to abuse any animal they might have had.

The shelter volunteer told them the shelter would close in thirty minutes. JD asked if he could complete an adoption form while his son met the dogs. That would allow the staff to clear him for adoption once Henry Kyle decided.

After agreeing that they could begin the process that way, JD waved his son off with the volunteer. He searched for a pen and took the clipboard with the application on it. Seeing a pen on the other side of the counter, and with no volunteer in sight, he reached over and snagged one. Then, he sat on the uncomfortable wooden bench to begin signing up for another lifetime commitment. This commitment didn't bother him one bit.

JD completed the form and handed it to a different volunteer, who had appeared to begin closing the shelter. She didn't seem happy that he waited until the last minute, but she input his application. Surely, they would approve it. He'd never been a pet owner before. Did that matter? He had no idea exactly what would qualify, or disqualify, him for the adoption.

The volunteer told him he could go find his son. After being directed to the dog kennels, he strode in that direction, slowly appraising each canine as he passed it. His heart broke, and he wished they could take them all home. He thought his food bill was high now; it must take a fortune to keep these hounds fed. He'd have to give them an extra donation. Maybe they could bring an extra bag of food each week. It wouldn't last long, but it would surely help.

When he stopped at the final kennel, panic set in. Where was his son? JD had walked through the entire dog kennel area, and his son was nowhere to be found. Rushing back to the front, to ensure the person he'd sent his son off with was indeed a volunteer, he caught sight of Henry Kyle. Fear rushed out in a heavy breath.

"Henry Kyle, you scared me."

His son turned around and smiled. "I'm sorry."

JD raised his eyebrows, staring at the pet his son held. Really? That was his choice? "Uhm, champ?"

"Dad, this is Cooper. I want to adopt him. He's been at the shelter the longest. It's time he found a home."

His son looked so happy; JD didn't want to burst

his bubble. "You're sure?"

With a confident nod, Henry Kyle said, "I know it's a cat, Dad, but I want Cooper, not a dog. I hope that's okay."

JD couldn't let his disappointment over not having a dog, even as an adult, damper his son's happiness. If he wanted a cat, by God, they'd have a cat. But.... He looked at the volunteer. "Is it true you should have two cats instead of one?"

The volunteer nodded. "It's better for their socialization, but not a requirement."

"Oh, Dad, I know the perfect one. It's a kitten. She's so loud and active."

They had come to the shelter to get a dog, and they were going to leave with two cats. "Let's go look at her." He heard a kitten meowing in the lobby. He hoped it wasn't that loudmouth.

And as one would expect, it was. Henry Kyle introduced him to Phoebe. The volunteer handed the kitten over, telling JD she was about seven weeks. He stilled. What was he to do with a kitten? The little one dug in her claws and climbed his shirt to his shoulder. There, she rubbed her forehead against his cheek, purring loudly. With that act, the little one stole his heart.

"Okay," he told Henry Kyle. "If they'll let us take them both home, we'll do it."

The volunteer said, "Cooper has been fixed, but you'll have to bring Phoebe to be fixed when she weighs three pounds. It's included in the adoption fee."

JD's mind whirled on what he needed to purchase for two cats. With a dog, he'd planned bowls and a bed. Didn't cats need more? Stuff to scratch on and climb?

What was he getting himself into? He'd never pictured himself as a cat person, but here he was....

Without crates, the cats were each put in a crate-shaped box with holes for transportation. He hated it for them but didn't want them running around in the car, either.

"Okay, champ, we're off to the pet store to buy some cat necessities."

"Can we bring the cats in with us? We can't leave them in the car." Henry Kyle looked worried.

"As long as we keep them in the boxes, we'll be okay bringing them in the store."

"You're all set," the volunteer said. "Congratulations on your adoptions, and thank you for the extra donation."

Just like that, JD and his son had two cats instead of a dog. It didn't seem to bother either of them. Hopefully, Cassie would fall in love with them as well. Thank goodness he didn't want their permission to marry her.

He hoped Henry Kyle would come around because he would marry Cassie at some point–agreement or not.

Chapter Eighteen

"You mean he chose cats instead of a dog?" Cassie asked as she stepped into JD's truck the following day after meeting at Coastal Investigation. Today, she'd donned a pair of dressy, black capris and a black and white blouse that she could imagine covered in cat hair. Cassie wouldn't care. A lint roller would take care of the mess easily enough.

JD closed the driver's side door. "He did. Surprised the hell out of me." He started the truck, then buckled his seatbelt.

"Truthfully," she said as she buckled her seatbelt, "I prefer cats over dogs, so I can't wait to meet them."

JD laughed and looked at her. "Apparently, so does my son." He leaned over and kissed her lightly on the lips. "Hmm. I could do that all day."

With her lips tingling, Cassie looked deeply into his eyes and noticed lust and disappointment. "You really wanted a dog, didn't you?"

He blew off the question with a shrug. "It doesn't matter. It's what Henry Kyle wants."

"True." Only, Cassie could tell it did matter. She remembered those early years when JD talked nonstop about wanting a dog, and his dad wouldn't allow it. It had probably been for the best because his dad tended to forget to feed JD occasionally. She could only imagine how well he'd care for a pet.

Putting the truck into reverse, JD turned, threw his arm across the top of the seat, and looked through the back window. "Thanks for changing my mind and attempting to schedule these appointments. I don't want to chase anyone around. We must help protect Missy since the FBI isn't worried about her, except to blame her."

Nodding, Cassie smiled. It'd taken some fast talking to convince him it would be easier for them. If the killer was a narcissist, he'd want them to speak with her and JD, so he could deceive them. If the killer were a psychopath, he may or may not want them to speak with him. Either way, it helped them make one appointment for the day.

"Yeah, at least we can meet with another beta reader. I'll try the one we missed on the drive."

They'd spoken with David Maynard, but hadn't been able to connect with Alex Finley. That could mean something, or it could mean nothing. Not everyone answers calls from unknown numbers. Plus, she hadn't left a message. She'd consider leaving him a message if she didn't get him on the next call–after they attempted to drop by his home again.

Tension flowed through the cab. Cassie couldn't lay her finger on it. It wasn't just because Henry Kyle picked two cats versus a dog. JD was chewing on something else that seemed to bother him deeply. She wanted to ask but knew they'd discuss it when he was ready. *If* he felt it was something to discuss with her. Cassie hoped his son wasn't giving him problems. JD and Henry Kyle appeared to be doing well.

Arriving at a brick home with a blue tarp on part of its roof, Cassie silently sighed as JD put the truck into park. The return trip had to be better. She'd felt on edge since his answers to her questions were short, along with his tone.

They sat in the driveway, quietly surveying the home. They'd arrived at a middle-class neighborhood that, while aged, was in good status, except for the roofs on a couple of houses. The most recent storm must have done more damage in this area than others.

A middle-aged, balding man opened both the front door and the hurricane door. He watched them, waved, and smiled.

"I'd say Mr. Maynard is excited to speak with us." JD unbuckled his seat belt.

Smiling and waving back, Cassie extricated herself from the truck and stepped lightly around the vehicle to meet JD. She'd worn heels and was glad for a paved driveway. They'd give her a problem at Mr. Finley's when they stopped by to see if he was home. Oh well, the black heels looked good, felt comfortable, and made her feel sexy. Any woman knew that was the trifecta of the perfect shoe. She simply had to wear them.

She only smiled at JD before turning to Mr. Maynard. No kiss. No handholding. No sexy glances. She hated it, but they'd agreed always to keep CI's image and reputation in tack.

"Mr. Maynard?" JD asked.

The man nodded. "Coastal Investigation? The ones helping Missy?"

JD held out his hand. "I'm JD Walker."

After they shook hands, Cassie offered hers. "I'm Cassie McKay. Thank you for taking the time to speak with us today, Mr. Maynard."

After shaking Cassie's hand, the man waved them

inside the home. "Please, call me David. Mr. Maynard was my father. God rest his soul."

Cassie immediately noticed the difference between Raymond Green's and David's homes. David had to have OCD because everything was neatly in place, looking as if measured to be aligned on the walls and shelves. Okay, he didn't have to have OCD to keep his house perfect for visitors.

Remember to listen and observe. Don't rush to a judgment without evidence.

The rules JD had drilled into her as a newbie came back to her. *Okay, open mind.* But one of these three had to be the killer. Were they in the home of a murderer? A chill crept down her spine at the thought. Why hadn't that same discomfort come over her in Raymond's home?

Cassie shook the fear off and focused on this interview. She could compare it later with JD.

The open living area was inviting, and Cassie could live in this home, even though it was possibly only a two-bedroom, and she wanted three. She really liked the three in JD's home. When would they discuss the next step? Maybe he was okay with things as they were and didn't want to move forward yet. Men were gun-shy at times.

"Sit. Sit," David said. "I want to help however I can. The FBI should never have targeted Missy. And believe me, when they spoke with me, they were after her and no one else."

Cassie didn't want to say that the letter most likely had caused a change. But she also hadn't spoken with the FBI to hear their thoughts.

Sitting on a gray sofa, Cassie and JD accepted a

glass of sweet tea. After David served them, he sat on a matching armchair. "Now, what can I do for you?"

JD asked some basic questions to confirm David's beginning with Missy a few years back.

"Have you ever met Missy?" Cassie asked.

David's eyes smiled. "I saw her at a book signing but haven't personally met her. We communicate through a beta reader app, email, and messenger. We don't meet face-to-face. When I first began with her, I lived in Michigan. I don't think she's realized I moved to Louisiana last year. Heck, I'm not sure if I told her or not." He shook his head. "I'll have to remedy that, or I'll never get my physical copy of her book. She always sends us a hard copy as a thank you for helping create the novel."

JD and Cassie looked at each other before taking sips of their drinks. Boy, oh boy, did David mean "sweet" tea. He had to have used more than the standard Southern one cup of sugar.

"What made you move here?" JD asked.

"It seemed a good place to retire. I was a police officer until I was shot in the line of duty." Obviously, seeing the change in their emotions, he waved them off. "Don't worry. I'm fine but didn't want to retake the chance. I wanted to live."

"That's right," Cassie said, "you started as Missy's police procedural expert."

Alex smiled and nodded. "Still am. I'm also a full beta reader. It's easier this way."

With her villain meter pinging, Cassie asked, "I don't think Missy said it, but how did you start with her?"

"I read her first book when it came out and noticed

she had a procedure wrong, so I emailed her and offered my services. After a bit, she asked me to beta read her new books to ensure the procedures were right and lead to the correct flow in the story."

That made perfect sense. Cassie wasn't a writer but knew some of Missy's challenges while writing. Her friend had called her frequently when she was in the FBI, asking for help. Not being a field agent, Cassie hadn't been the best person to assist.

"Look," David said, "Missy is perfect and needs you to prove her innocence, so the FBI doesn't railroad her. I don't want her to stop writing. Beta reading for her is about all I have going on in my life. Besides fishing, that is."

Fishing caught JD's attention, turning the two men's discussion to lakes, rods, and fish. Cassie zoned out on the boy talk. Oh, she did a bit of fishing, but not to the extent these two seemed to enjoy the sport.

She didn't know what to think. This man seemed like a nice man. He was fit, appeared healthy, and had time on his hands. He adored Missy in some semblance, but how, Cassie couldn't decide. Could he be their killer? *The ardent fan?*

As they prepared to leave, David left them with, "Let me know if I can help in any way. I don't have connections with the FBI, but I've made friends with the local police. They might find out something for us."

Cassie didn't like how he said "us" like he was part of the solution.

"Thanks," JD said kindly. "We'll call upon you should we need it."

Cassie thanked him also before she and JD entered the truck. After waving goodbye, he disappeared inside his home.

After buckling their seat belts, JD put the truck in reverse. "Strange fellow."

"Do you think he's our guy?" She leaned there but had no evidence.

JD shrugged. "I can't tell. We'll have to speak with him again, I think."

Confused, Cassie asked, "Why didn't you ask him more questions today?"

"He was too prepared. That's why I hadn't wanted to call. His answers were too perfect. I want to catch him off guard and see how he reacts."

She felt two inches tall after convincing him to call first. "Okay, I won't call Alex Finley then."

Turning briefly to her, he smiled. "Thank you, sweetheart."

On their return trip to Mississippi, they stopped at Alex Finley's. Again, the home was empty, almost as if it were abandoned. If Mr. Finley worked, they'd have to come either early or late one evening.

"Well," Cassie said, "we have two of the three interviewed, and I'm not sure we've got our man. Although some of David's answers spiked my villain meter."

JD glanced at her and laughed. "Villain meter? Is that a real thing?"

She swatted his arm playfully. "You know what I mean. He made me wonder if he was the killer, after all."

"Was it that he introduced his services to Missy? Or that he moved near her after retiring? Or that he seemed to love Missy, or at least the persona she presented?"

Cassie nodded and fingered a check in the air. "All of the above."

"What's wrong then?"

Sighing, she stared out the front windshield. "I guess I expected a more overt clue as to if he were our killer."

"It's possible he's not. Our missing beta reader may be the killer."

Thoughtfully, she replied, "True." After noticing JD's peculiar behavior, she asked, "Why do you keep changing lanes and checking the rear-view mirror? Are we being followed?" She wouldn't put it past Mike to follow them and devise an excuse to arrest them. Well, he'd arrest JD. He'd try to get her to go along with him and get back together.

"You didn't notice? That's not great PI awareness, sweetheart."

Cassie bit her lip. He was right. She hadn't checked her surroundings at all, except the passing scenery. "Who is it? Mike?"

JD shook his head. "No, it's Agent Angler. I noticed his car parked near Maynard's also. McKay probably sent him."

Beyond pissed, Cassie pulled her cell from her purse and scrolled to Mike's number. "I'm calling him. I'm done with this cat-and-mouse game." Okay, it wasn't really a cat-and-mouse game, but it was what came out of her mouth. When she got mad—really mad—her words didn't always make sense.

Dialing, she tried to put her words together before he answered.

"Hey, babe," he said smoothly, "are you ready to return to me and the FBI?"

The gall! "No," she firmly stated. "And I am *not* your sweetheart. You need to call off your dog. We don't need a chaperone while we help Missy."

"Dog? I don't know what you're talking about. Anyhow, we're no longer considering Missy as a person of interest. Although she is tied to the case, and we'll still be speaking with her since it is her book the killer acted out."

Okay. That took the wind out of Cassie's sails. "Good" was about all she could get out. Clearing her throat, she tried again, "Stop having us followed. We're not doing anything wrong. We're allowed to speak with any citizen we wish, especially if they are connected with our client."

"Look, Cassie, you're talking nonsense. I'm not having you followed. I've got better things to do with my FBI resources."

She narrowed her eyes. "So, you don't have Agent Angler following us?"

"No. That bastard is supposed to be chasing down Finley. We haven't been able to connect with him. Have you?"

"You know we haven't. Agent Angler followed us to Finley's home."

"Look," Mike said, "I sent Angler to check out Finley's home. Maybe it's a coincidence, and you arrived at the same time. Of course, he'd be on the same path back to Mississippi."

"But did you have him follow us to David Maynard's also?"

"No." Cassie ended the call. She turned to JD. "We've got a problem, and, for once, it's not Mike."

Chapter Nineteen

JD held his anger until he dropped Cassie off by her Jeep. That son of a bitch McKay was fucking with them. More like fucking with Cassie. JD wouldn't have it. He didn't believe McKay's lie about sending Angler to only Finley's. The bastard sent the agent to spy on him and Cassie.

JD slapped the steering wheel. It did nothing to control the rise in his temper. What was he going to do about that prick? JD expected should he step out of line that McKay would have him arrested—just to show his authority over Cassie. Would the man ever let her go?

Arriving at his home, JD sat outside momentarily, trying to turn his thoughts from the asshole. Instead, he surveyed his domain. JD had done well for himself and Henry Kyle. Much better than his old man had ever done for him.

All right, wrong direction of his thoughts. He had to have a diversion, and, unfortunately, Henry Kyle was staying the night with a friend. Usually, he wouldn't allow for school night stayovers, but since both boys were homeschooled, he was glad his son had found a friend through the homeschool organization.

JD wanted to slap himself. He'd meant to ask Cassie to stay over, but he'd been so pissed about McKay and Angler he'd forgotten entirely his happiness. Fortunately, Cassie was his happiness.

Along with Henry Kyle, of course.

Maybe he'd call her later—after he cooled off—and invite her over. They deserved a little off-duty time together, especially since his romantic night had been shot to hell.

JD turned back to his truck. Candles. Women loved candles, didn't they? He'd purchase a bunch of them and put them around the bedroom. Could he find rose petals that didn't cost his entire paycheck to sprinkle on the bed? Doubtful. Maybe next time.

After a rushed trip to the local superstore, he brought home twenty candles of all shapes and varying smells to light the bedroom. He hoped the scents didn't mingle to make a noxious smell. There weren't many choices, so he did the best he could at the time, trusting in the scent of roses, vanilla, gardenia, and white ginger.

Entering the foyer, he pulled out his phone to call Cassie. She answered on the first ring.

"Hello, handsome," she said.

"Hello, my sexy angel." Oh, he loved her playfulness.

"What's going on? Is everything okay with Henry Kyle? I thought he was staying with a friend. At least, that's what Mom told me."

Nodding, as if she could see it, he said, "He's staying with a friend, which is why I'm calling. I meant to ask you earlier if you'd like to come over, have dinner, and maybe stay the night."

"Hmm, what kind of dinner?"

Crap. He hadn't thought that far. He dropped the candles on the kitchen counter and opened the refrigerator. Nothing romantic. "How about takeout?

Your choice?"

She laughed. "Didn't get to the grocery store, did you?"

He sighed. She always figured him out. "No. That's a trip I take with Henry Kyle, so I get the 'right' foods he'll eat."

"So, Mac and cheese and pizza?"

JD laughed. "Basically." After a brief second, he asked, "So, what do you think? Me and you, alone, in the house? We can break in every room," he teased.

Cassie laughed. "Oh, you are feeling randy today. Tell you what, let me visit with Mom for a bit, then I'll pick up dinner and bring it over. How does that sound?"

That made his job easier, even though he felt guilty that she was taking care of dinner. "Okay, but it's my treat next time."

"Next time, you're grilling steaks for me." She ended the call.

Yes! He fist-pumped like he'd seen Henry Kyle do when he was excited. Tonight was theirs. He should have sent his son off to a friend's house before, but they'd been on the boat before.

Sniffing his underarms, he decided a shower was necessary. He swiped the bags of candles off the counter and strolled to his bedroom. After distributing them around the room, he stepped back and smiled. Seduction at its finest. At least, on his budget.

Ripping off his shirt, he tossed it in the laundry basket and stepped into his bathroom, leaving the adjoining door ajar for steam to escape. Turning up the tunes and the shower, he undressed, flexed to the mirror, realized he needed to go to the gym, and stepped under the warm stream of water.

As he washed his face, he decided he should shave–no sense leaving whisker burns on her silky skin. With the fog-free mirror in the shower, he quickly took care of his day's growth. Feeling the softness of his face, he nodded, deciding it would do.

Turning off the water, he reached out of the shower for the towel on the rack nearby. Wrapping the towel around his midsection, he stepped out on the rug and shook his head. Water flew everywhere. He chided himself for not doing it in the shower because now he would have to clean the mess. Oh well, later.

He took a hand towel off the counter and wiped across the steam-covered mirror. That's when he caught the gleam of candlelight from his bedroom. Crap, Cassie had beat him to the punch. When would he ever get it right?

Looking down, he realized he might as well greet her as is. It wasn't like he didn't plan to get naked later. He may as well get a head start. He did use the hand towel to wipe the water from his chest, arms, and underarms. Knowing he'd sweat during their lovemaking, he quickly reached out and picked up his deodorant, applying it liberally. Then, he sat the toiletry down and turned to his room. He pushed the door open and smiled.

"You made it already," he said then stopped dead in his tracks. It wasn't Cassie who had entered his house. Damn him for leaving the front door unlocked. *Lucy.* And, she had lit the candles and stripped down to a, he had to admit, sexy set of red lingerie.

"Hello, darling," she said from her seductive pose on his bed. She slid her finger over the swell in her breasts. "I was getting lonely waiting for you."

Oh hell no! This was not happening. Cassie was due, and she couldn't see this bitch in here, especially dressed like that.

Gritting his teeth to keep the lethal part of his anger out of his voice, he said, "What the hell are you doing here, Lucy?"

She pouted her perfect lips. Well, he'd always thought them perfect, then he remembered Cassie's lips where the top one was a bit smaller than the bottom. Oh, how he loved that imperfection in her otherwise perfect body.

"We haven't had time together because of that investigation you're doing. I thought I'd tell you that since my client has been dismissed as a person of interest, there is no need to continue. Then I remembered I wouldn't get to see you as much. So, we could discuss the case together. Over wine." She pointed to a bottle on the bedside table with two wine glasses that weren't his. Hell, he didn't even own wine glasses.

JD crossed his arms over his chest. "Get up. Get dressed. Get out of here."

When she climbed from the bed, he sighed in relief. Then, she asked, "Do you have a corkscrew? I forgot mine." After which, she strolled out of the bedroom before he could grab her.

Son of a bitch. JD looked to the ceiling. "Why me?" he muttered under his breath. He had to get her out of there before a nightmare occurred. Lucy was a she-devil. She was trying to cause problems with JD and Cassie so they could resume their sexual relationship. He just knew it.

Stepping out of the room, he followed Lucy to get

her to leave. Or at least get dressed. What the hell would he tell Cassie? The truth, of course. But would she believe him?

With Lucy in the kitchen and him midway through the living room, it was time to find out what Cassie would say because she knocked and opened the door. Entering, she smiled at him standing in the living room in a towel. She put down the bag of food in her hand and stepped toward him. "Nice," she said.

Then, the bitch had to ruin it all. She glided from the kitchen, like a sex goddess, purring, "JD, I can't find the corkscrew."

Cassie looked at her, looked him over, noting the towel again, turned, and slammed the door on her way out.

Fuck! Fuck! Fuck! JD raced from the house, holding his slipping towel. "Cassie, wait. It's not what you think."

When she turned, tears were in her eyes. His heart shattered into a million pieces. He hated to see her sob. No man should make a woman cry. "Exactly what was it?"

"She just came over."

"And you both got undressed? What, were you planning to have a quickie with her before I arrived?"

He reached out for her arm. She turned away. "No, Cassie. I was—"

"Save it, JD." She climbed into her Jeep and spun out, JD's heart going along for the ride with her.

JD watched her leave, noticed the neighbor watching him, and waved at the man. *Nosy asshole.* He had to take care of Lucy and make things right with Cassie. Surely, she wouldn't believe he'd mess up their relationship because of another woman. Then he thought of Susan. He hadn't broken up their relationship because of Susan, but Susan had been a rebound situation.

Turning back to the house, he walked through the open door. Lucy sat on the couch as if nothing had happened. "Are we alone, or do you have more visitors coming?" she asked.

"Get dressed and get the fuck out," he shouted.

Lucy looked at him, then at the open front door. A smile formed on her lips. "Sure thing, honey. But I'll be back. We have lots to revisit."

Revisit his ass. He knew he'd set himself up for a problem when he'd recommended her. JD never thought it'd be this horrible.

Chapter Twenty

Thunder woke Cassie the next day. Even with her blinds closed, she caught a lightning streak before another boom of thunder. Great. A day to match her depressed mood.

After pulling herself from the bed, Cassie looked in the mirror at her red, swollen eyes and wanted to call out sick. She couldn't face JD. He and Lucy had been all but naked. That didn't happen in an instant. Something had been going on whether he admitted it or not. What exactly, she wasn't sure.

Patricia handed her a cold compress. "For the puffiness."

Thankful her mother didn't say anything else, Cassie smiled, accepted the offering, and went to her bed. She lay down and put the compress on her eyes.

Lucy will be at the entire team meeting today. Cassie wouldn't allow herself to look less than stellar. While she couldn't beat the woman in looks, she could hold her own.

Today, they would discuss the case and whether to continue their investigation. The good thing was that Missy wouldn't need Lucy on retainer. In fact, why the hell had she been invited to the meeting?

She sighed. JD, of course. Something had told Cassie that he wasn't ready to settle down with her. It hadn't been a strong feeling, only a niggling doubt.

Now, it was monstrous.

After stretching for the umpteenth time, Cassie decided she'd had enough rest and got up from bed. She got dressed quickly and prepared to face the day. She wore one of her business suits from her time with the FBI analysis unit to build her confidence. She'd always felt strong and in control wearing a suit. And today she needed that boost.

The drive to Coastal Investigation didn't take long. She noted the Mercedes in the parking lot, and her ire rose when she arrived. That Lucy woman had already come. That brought back a thought she'd overlooked. Where had Lucy's car been the night before? It hadn't been in JD's driveway. Cassie guessed it could have been parked along the road, but she didn't recall seeing it. Had JD picked her up, or had she grabbed a ride? Hmm.... Something to ponder.

Knowing it was now or never, Cassie stepped from her Jeep, opened her umbrella, grabbed her purse, and strolled to the office, with her head high. So long as she didn't see JD and Lucy arm-in-arm, she could survive the meeting.

She was the last to arrive. Missy, Lucy, JD, Carl, Robert, Daisy, Gus, and Nan were there. It was good to see Gus today. He looked a bit peaked, but otherwise looked healthy.

Scanning the room, Cassie's gaze met JD's. He stood tensely, his eyes pleading. Cassie cut her eyes away from him. She couldn't deal with him right now. They had a case to discuss.

"Sorry, I'm late," she said, knowing she wasn't late but last. She sat at the table at one of the two empty seats. JD sat in the one next to her. Great. She could feel the heat emanating from him. Maybe it was just how her body reacted to his. Either way, it annoyed her. She refused to look at Lucy. She wanted to scratch the woman's eyes out for going after JD.

"Why are you still investigating when the FBI cleared Missy?" Carl asked as he pressed the record button on his cell.

Cassie knew the writer was ready to publish the next article about Missy and this case but had held back—at their request—while Missy had been a suspect. Darn reporters. She didn't have much use for them.

"Because," Missy said before anyone else could speak, "it might be one of my beta readers. If it is, I want the person found. I'd hate to think I'm giving a psychopath instruction to kill." Cassie's friend visibly shivered.

"You're not giving them instructions to kill," Cassie said soothingly. "It's just a psychopath using your book as an excuse to murder innocent people."

Robert, sitting beside Missy at the conference table, reached up and patted Missy's hand. "We'll figure this out."

Missy turned and smiled at him.

Cassie didn't like the way Missy's agent looked at her friend. Robert was besotted. How could no one else see the desire in his eyes? Then she glanced at Carl. Or the jealousy in Carl's? Poor Missy. It must suck to be a celebrity, of sorts.

"We must track down that last reader. I don't feel the other two are your killers, but we can give them another meeting." JD turned to her. "What do you think, Cassie?"

She thought she wanted to slap him but knew that wouldn't solve anything. One thing was for sure, she did *not* want to be in the car with him on a two-hour trip to Louisiana.

"I think the weather is too treacherous for the drive today. Besides, we're just hit-and-miss with Alex Finley. I think Missy needs to reach out to him via the app she uses to communicate with her beta readers."

"I tried that," Missy responded. "He didn't answer."

"Yes," Cassie said, "but did you give him something to critique or only a request to respond?"

Missy brightened as if she had caught Cassie's thought. "I see. I only asked him to respond. But I hate to send something new to him. What if he acts it out?"

"Send something simple. Something that won't put the crazy back in him," Cassie said. "And get him on regular email so we can get someone to track his IP address. Tell him"—she waved her hand, excited at her idea— "that you're changing service or it's going down, and you want to communicate via regular email in the meantime."

"*Bien, chere,*" Gus said. "Good. *Mais,* who track IP? We no tech people."

Cassie only knew one person who could help, and she couldn't ask him. Who, though?

JD launched himself from his chair. "If you're thinking of working with McKay, you're insane. I won't have it."

Utterly bewildered by JD's possessive statement, Cassie quietly turned and looked at his agitated self. "I am trying to think of someone else. I think maybe Levi can help. *And,* you have no say over me."

"Oh, no," Daisy whispered. "Lover's quarrel."

Cassie spun to the young woman and narrowed her eyes. She didn't want the people at work to get involved. Darn it. She knew a workplace romance never worked. Only, Cassie thought she and JD were different.

Daisy looked down. "I'll stay out of it."

As if noticing the tension between Cassie and JD, Nan took over. "Okay, Missy, you send a fake chapter and get Alex on regular email." She turned to Cassie. "You get with Levi and see if he can help or direct you to someone who can help." Then, she did the best thing ever, Cassie thought. Nan turned to Lucy. "You're excused. Missy no longer needs your counsel. Please don't return."

"Well, I never," Lucy said, taken aback.

Although she knew better than to gloat, Cassie smiled so broadly her face could have cracked.

JD, still standing, said, "She's right, Lucy. Missy doesn't need you any longer. There's no reason for you to be here."

"None?" the sexy attorney said as she stood. "I believe there is, but not at the meeting, so I'm off. I have more clients to see." As she breezed from the room, she ran her hand up JD's chest. "See you soon, lover."

Cassie almost jumped from the chair and belted the woman, but then she noticed JD didn't do anything to stop Lucy's touch.

In a childish move, Cassie scooted her seat further from JD's before he sat. It wasn't far, but it made a statement.

Carl spoke up. "This is turning into a real live case.

It's completely different from the expose I'm doing on Missy. Robert," he said, turning to the agent, "let's discuss how we'll present this to the public."

Robert nodded and stood. "Yes, we're done here, so let's catch an early lunch and get the articles moving."

As the two men left, both saying lovingly-type goodbyes to Missy, Cassie wondered if one of them could be Alex Finley. Then, she thought how stupid that would be. They weren't insane killers. They wanted nothing but the best for Missy.

"JD and Gus," Nan said, "you're excused."

The men looked taken aback. Gus, looking at Nan, eventually nodded as if he read his wife's mind. "*Bien, amour.*" He stood, leaned down, and kissed her cheek, then turned to JD. "Let's go, *cher.*"

JD appeared reluctant but stood and followed Gus to the back office. But not without a glance back at Cassie.

"Now," Nan said, "after you make the call to Levi, Cassie, call your mother. We're going to my house for a ladies night. It looks like we need it."

Cassie couldn't think of a better idea, especially since Lucy wasn't part of the ladies attending.

"That sounds like a grand idea," Missy said.

"Am I included?" Daisy asked.

Feeling bad about typically excluding Daisy from meetings and such, Cassie nodded and said, "Yes" before Nan could naysay the response.

"Since Gus might want to go home sometime," Missy said, "we can have the get-together at my hotel room. I have a suite. It's more than enough room for us all."

"That sounds marvelous," Nan said.

"I've got the catering," Missy said. When Nan and Cassie shifted to challenge her, she said, "It's part of my thank you for taking on this case. You can't say no."

"Well, all right then. I guess we're having a ladies night at the hotel." Cassie stood. "Let me chat with Levi, then I'll grab Mom and we'll be over." Now by Missy, she leaned down and kissed her cheek. "Thanks."

"I'm happy to do it," Missy responded.

Cassie knew the get-together wouldn't be about the case but about her and JD. Could she handle everyone having their say about the relationship? That brought to question where was their relationship? Maybe a few drinks and talking it over with friends would help her decide.

Chapter Twenty-One

"*Cher*," Gus said as he sat behind his desk in the back office. "What happen with Cassie? She more riled than a gator who miss his prey." Gus chuckled at his own joke.

Dropping in one of the armchairs across from the desk, JD sighed and rubbed his hand over his face. It didn't wipe away his distress for his relationship with Cassie. "She won't let me explain."

Gus raised an eyebrow. "Explain?"

After describing the night's events, JD sat, expecting some fatherly advice. Gus had always helped him with advice like his father hadn't, but they'd never talked about women before. With Gus and Nan married forever, it seemed the man should have some sound suggestions.

"She no take your call?"

No, she hadn't. He'd blown up Cassie's phone with calls and texts, and she'd not returned any, nor answered when he called. This meeting was his first sight of her since Lucy fucked up his life.

"Do romance, *cher*. Surprise her with flowers. Take her to dinner."

How the hell was JD supposed to do that when she wouldn't speak with him? He could show up with flowers but taking her to dinner hadn't worked the first time. In fact, it'd been horrible with McKay showing up. Which had JD's mind shifting to the case and McKay.

"Agent Angler followed us yesterday."

Going with the change of topic as if it was expected, Gus tilted his head. "Only him?"

"Yes. McKay says he didn't send him, but I don't trust McKay."

"He want your woman, *cher*." Gus shook his head. "He want her back."

JD knew this and wondered if Cassie would run to McKay after the fiasco with Lucy. Given their past relationship, he couldn't imagine her going to such extremes, but JD had to keep an eye on them.

"Who you think it be?" Gus asked, leaning back in his office chair, folding his hands behind his head in a relaxed pose.

"I'm betting on Finley since he's been so elusive."

Gus shook his head. "FBI no find Finley."

Not caring how Gus got the FBI info, since JD had blown up that bridge and set it on fire, JD replied, "Not good. Someone must have met this elusive beta reader. His landlord, maybe?" That would be the next place to look before going with Alex Finley as an alias, which JD was leaning toward since even the FBI couldn't find him.

"He buy on the computer," Gus told him. "Nan check already."

Great. JD's phone rang. When he saw Patricia's name, his heart raced. Was something wrong with Henry Kyle?

He answered as brightly as he could. Maybe he could get to Cassie through her mother.

"Hi, Patricia."

"Hi, JD. Before you panic, nothing is wrong with Henry Kyle. He's completed his lessons for today and is playing a game on the TV. I have a favor to ask."

Anything if it could get him in her good graces. "Sure."

"I understand you're calling the day early due to the weather. Can you, by chance, pick up Henry Kyle for the rest of the day? I've somewhere I'd like to go, and he would be out of place."

Patricia had never asked him to pick up his son early. In fact, he stopped regularly dropping Henry Kyle off because she picked him up and dropped him off each weekday. She said it got her out of the house. It helped JD, so he hadn't argued. Only now, he hated that it kept him from seeing Cassie more. Thinking Cassie would be there when he picked up his son, JD said, "No problem. I'll be there in a jiff."

"Thanks, JD." Patricia ended the call before JD could inquire about Cassie.

"I've got to run, Gus. I'm picking up Henry Kyle."

"He be okay?" Gus asked.

"Yes, Patricia had someplace she had to be."

Gus chuckled.

"What?" JD asked as he stood. "Is something wrong?"

"No." Gus shook his head. "Nan get *dames* together."

"A ladies night?" JD asked. "You're kidding. It's not even lunchtime."

Gus shrugged. "That it be. Pick up my godson. Speak with her."

"See you later." JD exited the office. He'd expected to find the women still in the outer office, but it was empty. Even Daisy had left for the day. Good grief. The weather wasn't so bad that they had to take the day off. Of course, he didn't want to travel to Louisiana in the storm either.

Hoping Cassie would be home when he picked up his son, JD stopped by the grocery store and bought a dozen red roses. Sure, it wasn't the flower store variety, but they didn't have a flower store in Gulf Islands. At least he splurged for the roses in a lovely vase instead of in plastic.

The drive to Cassie's was torturous for JD. All he thought about was how Lucy had screwed up their relationship and how Cassie wouldn't speak with him. He knew she needed cooling off, but he couldn't stand it. Eventually, she'd come to her senses and ask or let him explain. JD couldn't wait. His heart ached to be near her. To feel the heat from her body. To have her close to him, in and out of bed.

JD sighed heavily. He just needed her, period. He could resolve this. They'd been through worse. They could reconcile and marry. Marry? How was he going to convince Henry Kyle it was the right thing? JD couldn't allow his son to dictate his life, but something vital needed some buy-in from the boy. Otherwise, Cassie would have a terrible time with his son.

Arriving at Cassie's, JD pulled his truck into the driveway and paused before exiting. Cassie was home. He would make some time with her to apologize. Wait, why would he apologize? He needed to explain. Surely, she'd understand.

Putting on a baseball cap to keep the rain from his face, he carefully grasped the vase of flowers, exited the truck, and raced to the door.

Henry Kyle met him. "I'm ready, Dad."

JD would leave after he spoke with Cassie. "Hang on, champ. I need to speak with the grownups."

Henry Kyle glanced inside, then leaned forward to his father. "Are you sure?" he whispered. "I think Miss Cassie is mad at you."

Funny how his kid caught onto things so quickly. "I imagine she is, which is why I want to speak with her."

Moving out of the doorway, Henry Kyle rushed—because he never walked—to the couch with Patricia. "Miss Pat, I can play more." Then, he picked up a game controller and ignored the world around him.

JD shook his head. Did anything ever phase that boy? The shrink had done great things with Henry Kyle after the death of his mother. JD hadn't expected the boy to adapt so well, but JD's shrink had told him how resilient kids were.

Patricia stood from the couch. "Hello, JD. Beautiful flowers."

Henry Kyle, not stopping his fingers from flying over his controller, or his eyes leaving the TV, said, "If those are for Miss Cassie, she already got some today."

Taken aback, JD looked around and noted a dozen red roses on the kitchen table. He looked back at Patricia, and she appeared uncomfortable. It had to have been damn McKay. Now, he would talk with Cassie.

Cassie breezed from the back of the house and stopped when she saw him. After taking a moment, she moved forward. "Hello, JD. Those are beautiful flowers."

Handing them forward, JD fumbled with, "They're for you." She looked sexy in her tight blue jeans and plunging neckline blouse. They fit snugly but not like her painted-on jeans. Where was she going? He'd not seen her dressed this sexy before.

"Thank you." She took them and casually sat them on the table next to the other flowers. Maybe she was making a statement that other men found her attractive, or perhaps it was where she wanted to place them. JD had no idea, but he hated that she didn't speak.

Turning, Cassie smiled. "We're on our way out. Did you need something?"

Hell yeah, he did. He gritted his teeth. "Yes. You know we need to talk. It wasn't what it seemed. She came in and undressed while I was in the shower," he spouted out before she could cut him off or rush him. "I had no idea. I was trying to get rid of her when you arrived. I swear to you I didn't invite her, want her there, or have anything to do with her." Whew, that should cover it all.

The way Cassie stared at him made him fidget. Her not speaking right away crushed his heart and soul.

"We can talk tomorrow. Pick me up for breakfast," Cassie told him. She turned to her mother. "Now, we're leaving."

It hadn't been the answer JD wanted, but she was speaking with him, and they had plans for tomorrow. He'd figure out how to make her understand she was his everything.

"I'll see you at seven-thirty," he said.

She nodded, smiled, and turned. "Henry Kyle, we're leaving."

As Patricia grabbed her purse, Henry Kyle paused and saved his game. "Okay." He kissed the ladies on the cheeks. "See you tomorrow."

Now JD knew the boy listened, because it being Saturday tomorrow, Henry Kyle wouldn't usually have come to Patricia's. He wondered what else the boy had overheard that day. He knew it was wrong to grill his son on McKay's visit—assuming it was McKay. However, if his son told him any details, he'd take them.

"Come on, champ. Let's let the ladies get to their day." He had his chance tomorrow. He'd bring her dozens of daisies tomorrow, assuming he could find them in time. "We've got things to do ourselves." Like prepare for battle to win back a woman's heart.

Chapter Twenty-Two

Cassie wondered why she'd agreed to a day with the ladies. Her mood was so poorly that she figured she'd only bring them down to her level of upset. However, Nan had been insistent it would help her feel better. She hadn't agreed, but because Nan and then Missy pressured her, she was in the car with her mom, heading to the hotel.

"How are you, dear?" Patricia asked.

How was she? Sad? Lonely? Depressed? Feeling betrayed? All of those and more. "I'm fine."

Patricia harrumphed. "I doubt that."

"It's just…" She lost her train of thought. She was just what? "Okay, I don't want Mike to come back, and I want JD to have been telling the truth." There, she'd said it all in one breath.

"That's what I figured," Patricia responded. "I was glad to hear you give JD a chance to explain tomorrow."

Sighing, she shuffled her hands in her lap. She didn't fidget often, but when stress overtook her, she couldn't keep her body still. "After thinking about it, I can't believe JD would cheat on me. I think I was just so taken aback at the sight of them that I didn't think."

"That's usually how it goes."

Cassie didn't respond as they reached the hotel. They took the elevator to Missy's suite. After knocking on the door, Cassie realized they were the last to arrive. Nan, Daisy, and, of course, Missy were already there. Poor Daisy looked uncomfortable until she saw Cassie. Then, her eyes lit, and she rushed over.

"I didn't know what to say to her," Daisy whispered to Cassie. "It feels surreal being with her, just hanging out."

Cassie nodded. She and Patricia were welcomed with lots of "Hellos" and hugs. That made Cassie feel better. This might not be as bad as she expected.

"We're having mimosas," Missy explained as she took a fluted glass and drank. "You're welcome to them or Bloody Marys. If that doesn't work, I can have room service bring up whatever you like."

Cassie had yet to see the other suites at this casino hotel and was pleasantly surprised to find the room was much bigger than she expected. This must be a "high-rollers room."

"I'm driving, so I'll have water," Patricia said.

It wasn't hard to pull Cassie's arm. She loved mimosas. "I'll have a mimosa."

Once everyone had a drink in their hand, the women stood in a circle. Missy held up her glass in a toast.

"Here's to the great people of Coastal Investigation who have been an immense help," Missy said.

The women all raised their glasses, then drank. Knowing it was the right time, Cassie lifted her glass. "Here's to the best friend a woman could have and the best author around."

Again, they raised their glasses, but Daisy and Nan said, "Here, here."

"Brunch should be here soon. I ordered a bunch of

food so we can enjoy our day," Missy said. "If we need it, we'll have them roll beds in here for all of us to crash."

The women laughed. "Let's hope it doesn't get that far," Nan said. "This was to enjoy each other without the men and work."

"Here, here," Daisy said. When she saw no one else said a thing, she blushed. Cassie had not seen the woman when she wasn't confident and, for lack of a better word, dominant. She must be in absolute awe of Missy.

"How is Gus?" Patricia asked Nan. "I heard he was having problems."

Nan's smile faded, and Cassie wished her mother had not started this topic.

"He'll be fine, I'm sure," Nan responded. Then, she filled everyone in on the tests Gus had taken. They waited for the results to know whether a biopsy was necessary or whether it was nothing to worry about. "So, we wait."

"It's wrong they make you wait for those types of results," Missy said with a bit of anger, if Cassie guessed right.

"Well," Nan said, "we'll see it through."

"Now," Missy said, "what the heck is going on with you and lover boy?" she asked Cassie.

With the glass poised at her lips, Cassie hesitated before sipping. Then thinking better of it, she drank to give her time to formulate an answer. What should she tell these women? Besides Daisy, they were her friends. Daisy could be, she guessed, but they'd only talked about work before.

"Have a seat," Cassie said.

"Uh oh," Daisy said. "It's that bad?"

Cassie nodded. "Well, maybe not. I'm not sure."

"Let's sit at the table," Missy said. "There are more seats there than in the living room."

Although Cassie thought they could fit in the living room, three would have to sit on the sofa, making chatting awkward, so she followed Missy's suggestion. Daisy sat beside her, and Cassie wondered about this sudden friendliness from the office assistant.

Missy sat on the other side. "Now, spill."

So, Cassie did. She told them of finding Lucy at JD's half-naked.

"That bitch," Daisy said. "I knew I didn't like her."

"Didn't JD recommend her?" Missy asked.

The knock on the door interrupted the conversation and gave Cassie a short reprieve. Missy left the table and opened the door for the room service attendant as he pushed in a large cart with silver, dome-covered dishes.

Cassie's eyes almost bulged out of their sockets when a second room service attendant followed the first with another cart. Exactly how much food had Missy ordered? Were they expecting company? She hoped not.

As the attendants transferred dishes from the cart to the center of the table, Missy smiled sheepishly. "I may have ordered more than we can eat."

"You think?" Cassie said with a laugh that ended in a snort. "It's okay, we'll munch," she added after seeing the plates of fruits, especially strawberries with a cheese tray.

It took a bit for the attendants to finish and for everyone to serve themselves something to eat. Cassie chose a breakfast burrito with what, she wasn't sure, but hey, it was in a tortilla so how could she pass it up. Fruit and a cheese Danish pastry.

The women ate for a bit, talking about inane things until they began to refill glasses and push plates away. Cassie left part of her Danish because her tight jeans didn't have room. Dang it for wearing them to show JD what she offered compared to Lucy. That's what she got for being vain. But she'd enjoyed the rest. And the burrito had been sausage.

"Now," Missy said as she topped off Cassie's mimosa from the glass pitcher. "I'm glad I fired that bitch. She was a good attorney, but as a woman, I could have clawed her eyes out."

Everyone at the table nodded in agreement. Daisy asked, "What are you going to do? You two are so perfect for each other."

There had been a time when Cassie thought Daisy was after JD, but it had only been Daisy's possessiveness of her friendship with JD. Plus, she had tried to make Cassie jealous and run her away, but they'd settled that.

"I don't know. I agreed to meet him tomorrow for breakfast and discuss it." Oh, how she wanted just to throw her arms around JD and tell him how sorry she was. But what was she sorry for? According to him, she'd jumped to a conclusion. How could she not with them both half-naked?

Patricia opened another bottle of water. "Cassie received two dozen roses today."

Nan's eyes brightened, and she raised her eyebrows. "JD brought you two dozen roses? The boy must really be groveling."

"He should," Missy added.

Cassie sighed. Why had her mother brought Mike into the conversation? She'd kill her for it later. "They weren't both from JD. He did bring me a dozen red roses, but the other dozen was from Mike."

"Your ex? Mike?" Missy asked.

Nodding, Cassie stared at her drink. Why was Mike trying to get back with her? They'd been good together but not exceptional like she and JD.

Before she could respond, a knock sounded from the door.

"FBI. Open up," Mike McKay said from the other side of the door.

Chapter Twenty-Three

JD got a call he never expected to receive. Cassie rang him. "Mike is here to speak with Missy again. Can you get Lucy to Missy's hotel?"

His ire at hearing McKay's name dropped like a stone in a river when he realized her question. Cassie wanted Lucy? That must have taken a lot from her to ask that. But why was McKay talking with Missy again? They'd cleared her. "What does he want?"

"I don't know, but he won't let me sit in the discussion. Even though they cleared her, Missy won't speak with him without representation. I think she's scared they'll somehow blame her since she wrote the book."

"That's ludicrous," JD said. His mind whirred on defense attorneys. He would not, under any circumstance, call Lucy. She didn't deserve Missy as a client.

"I know," Cassie said, "but that's how she feels. I'd feel out of sorts also if I was her."

"Okay, I'll get someone there in a hurry." He ended the call and realized he hadn't said "Goodbye", "I love you", "I miss you", anything. He hit his forehead with his cell phone a few times to clear his brain. He had another thing to fix, but if Cassie's concern was Missy, that was his priority.

Frustrated, JD called the fifth attorney he knew.

Like the previous four, he couldn't get away immediately. Each attorney had an excuse like "I'm in court today", "I'm in a deposition today" and other attorney stuff that annoyed the hell out of him.

As he scrolled his contacts, JD stopped on one. He should have deleted the number long ago. Why hadn't he? *Because I'm a sucker, that's why.*

Figuring what the hell, he rang the number. Not a new attorney, but new to the defense side, he couldn't be as busy as the others he'd called. And even though he didn't want to speak with the man, he'd do it for Cassie. Hell, she'd swallowed her pride and asked for Lucy. JD could swallow his pride also.

"JD," Bryant Jacobs said.

Anger at Bryant's betrayal in sleeping with JD's ex while the two had still been together, along with the ire of the man knowing where his son had been and hadn't shared, flooded JD's system. This was a great deal of pride to swallow. Although, he wasn't trying to become friends again. JD needed the man's business service and that was it.

"Are you available right now?" JD asked gruffly.

"Sure. What's up?"

"You're needed as defense counsel at the Beau Rivage hotel for Missy Sauvage."

"The author?"

JD could hear the man moving around, hopefully grabbing his jacket to leave. "Yes. Oh, and Bryce, it's with the FBI."

"Well, when you call, you call. Fill me in on the drive."

"Call me when you're on the road." JD ended the call. He didn't want open air where Bryant could ask about their destroyed friendship.

JD also needed to get to the hotel, but he had Henry Kyle with him. With all the women there, he hoped Patricia or Nan would watch him while he worked.

"Champ?" JD shouted down the hallway.

When he heard no response, he yelled again. Nothing.

Damn Patricia for buying that boy headphones. He always had them on listening to music while playing games or wasting time on social media with his friends.

Entering the boy's room, JD took a whiff. Good grief, it smelled like a locker room. Maybe they needed a part-time cleaning lady. Or perhaps he could also get his son to start cleaning up himself. The kid was old enough to keep the room neat and smelling good.

Those were thoughts to tackle another time. When Henry Kyle saw him, the boy pulled the headphones from his ears to around his neck. "What's up, Dad?"

"We need to leave. Can you be ready in a few minutes?"

Henry Kyle jumped up from the bed. "I just need to put on my shoes, and I'm ready."

Bryant called before JD and Henry Kyle got on the road. Juggling the call, his son, and his concerns about McKay being near Cassie, JD entered and started the truck.

"Give me a minute," he told Bryant.

JD turned to his son. "When we're there, you must remain with Miss Patricia or Granny Nan. Do you hear me?"

Henry Kyle smiled and nodded. "Sure thing." Then, the kid put the headphones back on his ears.

147

JD shook his head. As they cruised down Highway 90, JD filled Bryant in on all that had occurred concerning Missy and the FBI case. He wasn't specific about the missing beta reader, but he alluded to the fact that they'd hit a dead end on the case before ending the call.

JD and Henry Kyle pulled into the Beau Rivage Hotel, and JD chose valet parking. He generally didn't utilize the luxury because he liked to walk in the fresh air, but he needed to get upstairs as quickly as possible. Cassie needed him. And McKay was there.

"Is everything okay?" Henry Kyle asked him in the elevator.

JD studied his son. The boy was sprouting up like a weed. Before long, he'd be as tall as JD. "Everything should be fine. It's that Miss Missy needs our help."

"I like her. She's nice."

JD nodded. Cassie had found a friendly and thoughtful woman to be her friend. Even though they hadn't been close lately, it was clear they were still close if someone saw them together.

The elevator opened and they exited. Immediately, JD spotted Cassie at an open doorway. He gestured for his son to follow him.

"Whoa," Henry Kyle said when he saw the hotel suite. "This is huge."

"Champ, what did we discuss?"

Henry Kyle nodded. "Stay with the old ladies and stay out of trouble."

JD couldn't believe what his son had said. Obviously, neither could Cassie because she corrected him before JD could. "It's not nice to call people 'old ladies.'"

Henry Kyle shrugged. "All right." Then he went to Patricia, who nodded to JD before she gave the boy her full attention.

"Now," JD asked as he and Cassie stood in the doorway, "what's happened since we spoke?"

"Well." Cassie drew out the word. "Bryant is in with Mike and Missy." She watched him closely. "Bryant? Really? I can't believe you called him of all people."

JD shrugged. "I figured it was better than Lucy."

Cassie smiled at him. So, he'd made the right choice to avoid Lucy. Score one point for his comeback. He only wished he'd had time to pick up daisies.

"Look, Cassie," JD said, peeking into the room to see if anyone was nearby. "Can we talk? I don't want to wait until tomorrow."

After looking inside, Cassie ushered him into the hallway and closed the hotel room door behind her. "Listen, JD," she started then stopped.

He waited, but she didn't say anything else right away. He wanted to jump in and apologize but knew she had something she wanted to say first. No matter how much it killed him, he'd wait.

"I'm sorry," she finally said.

JD straightened. Why was *she* sorry? "Cassie, you have nothing to be sorry about. I'm the one who is sorry. I am kicking myself for not locking my door so that–that conniving bitch couldn't have entered." He clasped Cassie's upper arms lightly. "Nothing happened. I didn't want anything to happen. I just wanted her gone."

"I realize that now." Cassie smiled up at him, and

JD's pulse accelerated.

Scrunching up his brows, JD asked, "You do?" Did that mean they were back together? Good grief, relationship stuff stumped him.

In a move any high schooler would love, Cassie slid her arms around his neck and pulled his face down to hers. When their lips nearly touched, she whispered, "I do."

Then she kissed him.

"Good God," Mike McKay said when he walked into the hotel hallway. "Cassie," he demanded, "I need to speak with you. Alone."

Cassie reluctantly let go of JD, pulling her lips away from his. Her hold on him slowly released. She and JD shared a gaze that she imagined said, "Why couldn't her ex-husband go away?"

Stepping aside, but remaining close to JD, she looked at Mike. "What can I do for you? Where's Missy? Is she okay?"

Looking perturbed, Mike said, "She's fine. Now, about that alone time."

JD put his arm around her shoulder, and she sank into him. "You no longer get alone time with her. If you want to speak with her, then you speak with me also."

Cassie's heart swelled with love and pride at JD's statement. Then it crashed with Mike's.

"Oh, but I'm FBI."

Nodding, JD said, "So you've said. Many times. Get a warrant if you want to speak with her as FBI."

Mike bristled. "I don't need a warrant to speak with my ex-wife."

"No, you don't. But, if you plan to speak with her alone, you're mistaken."

Cassie had had enough of the two alphas. "It's okay, JD. I can speak for myself."

JD tensed beside her. Did he think she was going to side with Mike? Oh, she hoped she hadn't given him that impression.

"Mike, JD comes along if you want to speak with me. We have no secrets." That wasn't entirely true, but close enough for Mike's knowledge.

Mike narrowed his eyes at Cassie. "Really? So, you've told him we offered you a slot in the next FBI academy class?"

JD didn't flinch as Cassie had expected at the news. No, she hadn't told him that, but bless his heart, JD acted as if she had to show Mike they were that close.

"What do you want?" she asked.

Mike checked his watch, as if bored. "I want an answer…to both of my questions."

Frozen, Cassie knew to say "No thank you" but the words didn't come fast enough. As she formed the first word, JD spoke up.

"No thank you," he said. "She's fine where she is."

"Is that true, Cassie?" Mike asked.

This time, she flaunted her courage. She nodded and said, "It's true. I'm not interested."

"We'll see," Mike said before he walked off.

Cassie and JD watched him step into an elevator before they moved. "I'm sorry," she immediately said. "He's such a pain."

"We have much to discuss," JD said. "But let's get to Missy."

Missy. Oh crap. She'd forgotten her friend. How horrible was she? "Right." Leading the way into the hotel room, Cassie rushed to a crying Missy. "What's wrong? Did Mike make you cry? I'll kick his butt for that."

Missy chuckled amid her tears. Using a tissue, she wiped them away. "Don't make me laugh. It's so sad."

Cassie sat beside Missy on the sofa. "What's sad? What happened?" Her heart couldn't handle anything wrong with Missy.

"He killed the final person–like in my book."

Chapter Twenty-Four

My work is done...for now.

There are no more deaths in the book except for the villain. I'm smarter than that killer, and Missy has shown me what that character did wrong, so that I can avoid the mistakes.

In the book, the hero ends up with the heroine. In our love story, I end up with Missy.

As I recall last night, I think of my heart pounding as I left the victim's home and a cop pulled up behind me, lights flashing. I know they cannot be onto me. I don't worry. I'm that good. As the cop sped by, I laughed and gave a mock salute to the departing officer. The police had a serial killer that close and didn't capture me.

I sit in my Louisiana home's living room armchair today and sigh. What will be my next step? My plan was to launch Missy to the top of the charts to prove my love for her. She's already #2 in the *New York Times* bestseller list. Surely, I've done enough to show her I'll go to the ends of the earth for our love.

My patience is nearing an end. I thought I could wait to declare my love, but now I'm unsure. I know she'll be number one after this final murder is made public. Why wait? It's only delaying the time we could spend together.

While it hasn't been announced outside our weird

circle of FBI, PIs, and entourage, my love has heard of the final murder on *Cross My Heart*'s list. How long will we keep it silent from the rest of the world? If that prick McKay decides to hold back the final murder, I may need to anonymously leak it to the media to expedite Missy and my moment of unity.

I leave the living room to get ready for the day. After I brush my teeth in the bathroom, I stop and look at myself in the mirror. I already know I look good, but not this damn good. Missy is a lucky woman to have all of this and my love.

Missy is a great person who exudes sex appeal. She doesn't realize it as she doesn't use it to help sell books. She is perfect for me. I remember the day I saw her on the back of a book cover and knew we were meant to be together. I love this woman with all I am.

I see her so often now that my cock aches to be inside my love. I can barely wait until I can undress her toned body and see what lies beneath the lovely clothes she wears. In the mirror, I watch the bulge in my pants grow as I think of ways to dress and undress her. Oh, what a beautiful woman, my Missy. We're so close to being an official couple.

Unfortunately, she doesn't plan to submit another book until I'm caught. That will not happen. I will not allow her to stop writing. Missy is talented, and the world knows this. They crave her work—as do I. Nor will I be caught. In the end, Missy will not allow it. When I admit who I am to my love, once I explain, she'll agree to keep our secret and write more. I'll always act out any book she wishes to boost sales.

I walk to the kitchen for breakfast. A thought occurs to me as I drink bottled water in the tiny room.

Will Missy believe me when I tell her all I've done for her? I didn't take pictures or souvenirs to prove it. That would have left a potential for me to get caught. I'm not that stupid. I didn't leave behind any clues like in the book. Those steps I knew to skip.

How will I prove my devotion? *Think...think...think....*

As I pace my small space, I realize she must know of my double life. I don't have any proof of that either. We've never written personal emails, only working in the app for beta readers. And I covered my tracks using coffee shops and public WIFIs as much as possible.

She did ask for me to email her personally, but I knew that was a trap. Did they really think I was not in the know? I'm right there with everyone—the FBI and Missy's team. And no one has noticed. I knew I could get away with this.

After I show Missy my small house in Louisiana—to prove my double life—I'll take her to my home in Mississippi. Then, we can continue as a couple and carry on with our professions like nothing happened.

No one will be the wiser. Oh, they'll wonder about the two of us, but we can say circumstances brought us together. It happens all the time when two people spend more time together than usual, especially during a traumatic part of their lives. Besides, we're both beautiful people who tend to gravitate toward each other.

My cell buzzes with a text. Hmm, McKay wants a meeting with the FBI, Coastal Investigation, and Missy's team. What's his angle? He's insisted that little investigation agency stay out of his way.

McKay is out to get his ex-wife back, so he must

be trying to impress Missy and her by including them. Or, and I laugh out loud at this, he's stumped. I take joy in outwitting that asshole. He needs a few pegs taken out of his stride.

Can I help in that task? I know it bothers Missy that her best friend is dealing with her ex-husband and not enjoying it. I'll have to consider that and see how my love deals with McKay.

I check my watch and realize I must ignore that problem for now. I need to get to Mississippi for the meeting, pronto. I'm glad they gave us two hours because it will take me that time and maybe more to get there and be in character.

Locking up the house, I take the time to wipe down all the surfaces I'd touched that day. I never rush out without doing that. Unfortunately, I also didn't have time to vacuum, so I hope I didn't lose any hair follicles today.

In the car, I look at the home I used to be Missy's pawn. I no longer need it. Indeed, she'll not need this home to believe me. Why wouldn't she believe what I told her? She trusts me now, so why not later?

I slap the steering wheel. I know better than to leave the home at this point, especially without a thorough cleaning. The FBI is too close. It's about warrant time.

Knowing I will probably be late, I take the chance and get out of the car. It's time I get rid of this part of my life and move forward as Missy's future husband.

I had planned this and had the fuel to spread over the floors and walls. It takes less time than I expect before a tiny flame sparks. Being out in the country, neighbors won't see it until it is engulfed. I don't need to wait to ensure my work is complete.

Back in the car, I smile at my handiwork.

As I back out of the dirt drive, I take one last look over my shoulder. It'd been fun while it lasted. However, it had been incredibly lonely. No more time to think about what was. I need to rush to Mississippi, to attend a special meeting, and the only woman who holds my heart.

Soon, Missy, we'll be together in all ways.

Chapter Twenty-Five

Cassie sat with Missy at the Coastal Investigation office boardroom table, filled with happiness and trepidation. Joyful in the knowledge that she and JD had cleared the air. It had been the Lucy woman she hadn't trusted, but it'd come out all wrong. No matter. Things were now right with the two of them.

The trepidation came from this meeting Mike had called. Why had he decided to include CI in his investigation? Unless he was here to rip them a new one yet again, this time as a group, including Robert and Carl, who were both late. Then again, so were Mike and the rest of the FBI group. Knowing Mike's regard for punctuality, she couldn't imagine what was keeping him.

The door flew open, and she jumped. Agents Angler and Miles strode in, both looking a bit harried. The wind outside kicked around, and Agent Miles's hair flew around her face. Agent Angler looked wildly around the room. Mike McKay and his intolerance for tardiness would do that.

The two agents nodded and took up positions by the door. "Special Agent McKay had a meeting and will be running a bit behind," Agent Miles informed the group.

Nan, not one to allow people to call her office inhospitable, offered them coffee. Both accepted, which shocked Cassie. She bet they wouldn't have if Mike had been there.

Cassie sipped her coffee, pondering where the men had gone, including JD, who wanted to bring Henry Kyle to see his Aunt Cece who was in town for a visit.

Missy nervously twiddled with a pen in her hands. "Do you think he's going to include you now?" she whispered to Cassie.

Shrugging, Cassie reached across and held down Missy's moving hand. "No matter. You know we're here for you. He doesn't think you did this."

Missy nodded and sighed. "I know. It's just—I wrote this lunatic a roadmap."

Cassie empathized with her friend, but couldn't understand the depth of Missy's emotions since Cassie had never experienced such a situation. She wasn't one to say I know how you feel when she didn't. That was patronizing. And she hated it when people did that to her.

Moving her hand away, Cassie gave Missy a nod. "We'll get through this together. Now—" she sat straight in her chair and raised her voice to an average level "—where are these men of yours?"

It warmed her heart to hear Missy giggle, even for a moment. "They're not my men, but both are on the way."

As if manifesting from their conversation, the two men walked into the office, deep in conversation. They looked up and around until they caught Missy's eye and nodded, still chatting.

JD strode into the office, the wind pushing the door open before him and slamming it against the wall. His eyes widened. "Sorry, Nan," he said without looking around.

As if knowing exactly where Cassie was, he strode to the table, kissed her on the top of the head, and dropped beside her. He nodded at Missy. "How are you holding up?"

"About as good as can be expected, I guess," she said.

Cassie caught JD searching the room. "Gus is in the back," she said. "Mike's not here." Surely it had to be one or other piece of knowledge he sought.

JD stood. "I'll be right back." He walked toward the back office to Gus, while everyone else remained at the table.

"What do you think McKay wants?" Carl asked as any greedy reporter would.

It occurred to Cassie that Carl and Robert might now know about the last murder. Is that what Mike wanted to share? Well, she wouldn't burst his bubble and tell them ahead of time.

Missy broke down. "I can't believe this is happening."

Robert and Carl, on each side of her, turned to Missy, while Agents Angler and Miles watched with narrowed eyes. Did they suspect the men? Surely not.

"Oh, Missy," Robert said and patted her hand.

Carl, not to be outdone, patted her other hand. "You can't allow this to get you down. You've done nothing wrong."

Robert snarled at Carl. "Of course she hasn't, and don't you dare print otherwise."

Oh-kay. The men needed to get along better. Then again, Cassie hadn't seen many who did get along well with reporters on the job.

Before anyone could respond, JD and Gus walked up front. Cassie was shocked at how peaked Gus looked. He walked firmly though, so she was optimistic the situation wasn't as severe as it seemed.

JD shook his head and smiled at Cassie. *Thank God, no cancer.* The news didn't get better than that.

Gus walked to Nan and sat beside her. "*Mi amour,* who we wait for?"

"Mike McKay," Nan said as she stood, went to the coffee pot, poured a cup, and brought it to her husband.

Gus looked at the coffee as if it smelled terrible but thanked his wife. "We no need McKay," he added as he pushed the coffee away. So, his stomach still bothered him. Maybe an ulcer? Cassie couldn't wait to find out from JD.

"We solve this," Gus added.

Agent Angler cleared his throat. "With all due respect, Mr. Fontaine, the FBI will solve this. Mike wants to ensure everyone is on the same page."

The door opened, and Cassie expected Mike, but saw Bryant Jacobs enter.

He smiled. "Sorry, I had to clear my schedule for this." He looked around and sat in the only available chair, beside Cassie.

Cassie had yet to forgive Bryant for all he'd done to JD in the past. She couldn't believe JD would go to that extreme to keep Lucy from their midst. It told her how much JD loved her. She wondered what conversation had happened between the two men and was anxious to find out later once she and JD were alone.

JD leaned over to her and whispered, "Still feeling those mimosas, my love?"

Had that only been a few hours ago? Cassie's mind was clear and sharp with another murder on the table. She knew they weren't the primary investigation unit, but she would be involved in any way she could to help her friend.

Cassie shook her head to answer his question. "How was Cece?" she whispered back, as if they couldn't converse on personal matters out loud.

JD leaned back in his chair and responded, "She was good. Happy to see Henry Kyle. She's moving back. I guess the new job isn't all it was cracked up to be."

Luckily, Cassie's transition from the FBI to the private sector, relocating from Virginia to Mississippi, had been both rewarding and swift. She wouldn't change either.

The wind whistled outside before the door opened once more. Mike had finally arrived. Looking around the group, his eyes stopped on Cassie.

She gulped and looked away. Let him leave her group alone today.

Instead of apologizing for being late, Mike said, "Good, you're all here." He moved to the table, saw no empty chair, and grabbed Daisy's from behind her desk, dragging it over until everyone turned to him.

Poor Daisy missed this meeting. She left straight from the hotel to the University of Southern Mississippi where she took weekend classes. Nan refused to allow her to attend work on a school day. Cassie promised to tell her everything.

"As you all know," Mike began, "we've had another murder."

Robert and Carl started. "What?" they said almost

in sync.

Looking surprised, Mike looked at Missy. "I assumed you would've told them."

Missy shook her head. "You said to keep it quiet."

Mike nodded. "So, for all of you to be informed, there was a fourth murder in exactly the same style as Missy's book."

It surprised Cassie that Mike told them—CI and Missy's team—that it happened exactly as it had. Maybe he held back something. She wanted to know but also wanted to avoid Mike as much as possible. But, to help her friend, she'd do what it took.

"Since no one at this table will stay out of the way, I've decided to bring you into the confidence of the FBI." He looked at Robert and Carl. "And this will not be used in print or press releases," he emphasized.

The two men he addressed nodded.

"All right," Mike continued, "we're all moving in the same direction and to keep from stepping on each other's toes—" which Cassie took as them stepping on Mike's toes "—we'll work together, to a point."

Cassie took that to mean they'd work together until it was time to make the arrest and get the glory. Those were reserved for Mike. She didn't care if it helped get a crazy man off the streets and out of Missy's life.

"We've all narrowed our list down to the beta readers. Raymond Green and David Maynard are clean and no longer suspects."

How had Mike completely cleared them? Indeed, she and JD didn't suspect them, but they hadn't turned their backs on them.

"Alex Finley is an alias."

Well, that explained that. It was what JD had

suspected but CI had yet to prove.

Missy gasped. "You mean I've been working with someone who lied about themself?"

Mike nodded. "Sorry to say so."

Cassie noted Missy's hands shaking. "How did you find out?" Cassie asked to keep everyone's notice from her friend.

"That's FBI business," Mike said with a bit of surliness.

There was the Mike that Cassie knew. All asshat to others. At least he'd brought them to the table for most of the information.

Mike's cell rang, and he grumbled as he pulled it from his pocket. He silenced the call and put the phone back in his pocket. "Now," he said.

His phone rang again, and he closed his eyes for a moment. "Hold on." He yanked the phone from his pocket, and with a shortness to his voice, answered, "McKay."

Mike's eyes narrowed as he said several "Uh huhs" into the phone. Once he disconnected, he looked around the room. "I came here to tell you that our warrant came back approved to go through Alex Finley's residence."

That shocked Cassie. Mike must really be certain it was Finley, or whatever his true name was.

"However," he said, and a muscle jumped in his jaw, "his home in Louisiana was burned to the ground this afternoon."

"What does that mean to us?" JD asked.

"That means," Mike stared at JD, and then stood, "we're through sharing."

Chapter Twenty-Six

"I've had enough of that son of a bitch," JD said after Mike and his FBI agents left Coastal Investigation. "He's jerked us around too many times."

Nearly salivating, Carl said, "This is turning out to be a better story than I expected."

Robert leaned around Missy. "Don't you dare print any of this." He tugged on the edge of a jacket sleeve. "At least, not until we ensure Missy is free and clear. Not even a person of interest."

Carl frowned. "But—"

"No buts," Robert said. "We have a contract requiring my approval on anything you print."

"In the newspaper," Carl said. "But this is novel worthy."

"It's already a novel, you idiot," Robert spat.

As Robert and Carl continued to argue, Missy stood and walked to Cassie and JD.

"What do you think?" Missy asked.

"Well," Cassie said, "he gave us a key piece of information we suspected but hadn't confirmed."

"That it was an alias?" Missy asked.

Cassie nodded. "Yes."

Missy shook her head. "I feel like such a fool. Alex had given such great feedback; I would never have guessed he took it to heart. And why now?"

"That's my question," Nan said as she and Gus

stood.

"I think he finally snapped," JD answered. "The fire shows he's trying to cover his tracks. He thinks he can get away with these murders."

"We'll leave you to this," Nan said as she and Gus walked to the back office. "We'll make some calls."

Missy sat in Nan's vacated chair. "Is it possible Alex is a woman? I mean, we never met."

JD thought for a moment. "It's always possible, but with the strength to strangle the women, I suspect a man."

Missy nodded. "I'm going to at least Zoom with my beta readers from now on."

Cassie stretched her neck from side to side. "It probably wouldn't matter. If this is someone who survived this long with two lives, he may have fooled you, anyhow. Psychopaths find it easy to show people what they want to see."

JD stood. "Let's find this bastard and show Mike he can't fuck with us like this."

"What happened to watching the language for Henry Kyle's sake?" Cassie chided.

"That asshole brings it out in me."

"Don't let him get to you like that," Cassie said. She and Missy also stood.

"Don't let who get to you?" Robert asked as he and Carl joined them.

JD shook his head. "Nothing."

Missy fidgeted. "Are you sure you want to do this? I mean, it's okay now. They don't suspect me of anything. I'd hate for you to get into trouble with the FBI."

Laughing, JD said, "It won't be the first time for

me."

Cassie frowned. "It will be for me." She looked at Missy and nodded. "But you're totally worth it."

"Do you want to hand out assignments?" Robert asked as if he were part of the investigative team.

JD raised an inquisitive eyebrow. "Hand out assignments?"

"Yes," Carl said. "We want to help too."

Robert turned on Carl. "You only want a better story."

"What's wrong with that? It's my job, after all!" Carl bickered.

"Stop it," JD nearly shouted to the two men. He'd tired of their constantly arguing over the damn articles or expose´ or whatever Carl was writing about Missy. It seemed that he was around all the time for only a few lines in any newspaper forum.

Well, he may as well keep the two men busy to get them out of his way and Missy's way. "Okay, Robert, go back through Missy's book and see if we missed anything that might point us to a clue to the killer's identity." It was a shot in the dark, but so be it. "Carl," he turned to the reporter. "Stay here for a moment. I have a special task for you." He'd use the man's contacts to their benefit. Or, at least to Cassie's benefit.

"Cassie," JD continued, "time to call Levi back and see what else we can get from the FBI before he's out of the loop."

Cassie nodded and walked off, pulling her cell from her pocket.

"What about me?" Missy asked.

"You can help me," Robert said. "With two of us, we can go faster, plus you'll remember things I miss."

Robert had a good point, so JD agreed. "We'll meet back here tomorrow morning."

The remaining group members split off while Carl remained.

"What can I do for you?" he asked JD. "I have lots of contacts that could help."

"Do you have any with the FBI in Quantico?"

Carl nodded. "A few."

"Good. This is what I want from you." JD explained the task, and Carl smiled.

"You can count on me." Carl executed a mock salute.

"And, Carl, this is between us."

Nodding, Carl grabbed his messenger bag from the table and headed to the door. "Of course."

JD wondered if the man would keep it secret until it was time to reveal his task. He could only hope and trust. Ha, trust a reporter. What the hell had he been thinking?

Cassie walked back into the room. She appeared ecstatic yet nervous.

"What's wrong?" he asked. He worried something had happened to Gus since Cassie had been in the back of the office. Maybe she'd heard something about his health.

"Levi's on vacation," she said.

"Well," JD responded and sat, pulling her onto his lap, "that sucks."

Cassie wrapped her arms around his neck. "Actually, I got in touch with him at home."

"Oh." He pushed a few strands of her hair behind her ear. "Can he still help?"

"That's my news. He's coming here to help."

JD almost dumped her from his lap as he stood. "What?"

"Yeah, he wants to help and figured since he's off, he'd just visit."

JD's jealousy roared loud and clear. He'd not met the man, and Cassie had said he was older, but the two flirted outrageously. What if Levi was after Cassie's heart?

"I think I've convinced him Mom is for him, and he wants to meet her."

"Huh?" That threw his mind for a loop. Her mother? "But—"

"I know," she said and kissed his cheek before she stood, "he's a bit eccentric, just like her."

JD couldn't deal with that part of Levi's visit. The tech guru could be of benefit, however. "When will he be here?"

Cassie shrugged. "I'm not sure. He was going to make his flight reservation after we spoke. I'd bet later today or in the morning. It depends if he decides to fly here or into New Orleans."

"He should get a flight into New Orleans today." JD stood, adjusting himself from where Cassie had sat on his lap. He needed time with her, alone. But it'd have to wait at least, until tonight.

"Let's go see if there's anything left of Finley's home."

Cassie's eyes widened. "Mike will be there, and he won't be happy."

"I don't give a—"

She arched a brow at him.

"Fig," he substituted.

Cassie laughed. "Let's tell Gus and Nan we're

leaving."

JD playfully swatted her behind. "Let's."

After their goodbyes, they jumped into Cassie's Jeep and traveled to Louisiana and Finley's residence.

"You know," JD said carefully, "I am beginning to believe—" well, he'd believed for a while but hadn't wanted to tell Cassie, "—that this Finley could be close to Missy. Especially now that we know it's an alias."

"What do you mean?" she asked. "Do you think it's Robert?"

JD shrugged as he grabbed the "oh shit bar" when Cassie swerved to pass another car. He knew he really should have driven. While she'd never been in an accident, she drove a little too close to other vehicles for his preference.

"Or, Carl," he added.

"Hmm."

Cassie was quiet momentarily as she stopped at a red light behind an 18-wheeler. Almost under the semi-truck, but JD knew better than to say anything. She was touchy about her driving abilities.

"What do you think about Agent Angler following us that day? Do you think it could be him?" Cassie asked.

JD shrugged. "We're really speculating. It could be just about anyone, but I'd bet my left nu—"

Cassie turned to him, and he rethought that statement.

"I'd bet my house he'd want to be close to her right now."

"That's something Levi mentioned," she told him.

"What? You're just now telling me his thoughts?"

"Well, it wasn't something I thought about until

now. We'll know better once he arrives. He is the best analyst at the FBI."

"You were a great analyst too. Why aren't you analyzing this case?"

"I am," she said. "I just don't have enough data. We need a data expert at the office. Someone who can access data elsewhere."

"Can Levi help while he's here?"

Cassie nodded and looked in her rear-view mirror. "Oh yes. He plans to bring his laptop."

"Well," JD said as he thought, "we can't rule out the entire world, but we can rule out those close to Missy."

"Dang it. We should have done that first."

"Don't beat yourself up, Cassie. We thought Finley was a real person. I mean, he is, but he's not Finley."

As they arrived near Finley's burnt residence, they were diverted by the police. Nothing they said could get them through the roadblock.

"Mike planned for us, didn't he?" she asked.

"It appears so." JD thought for a moment and brightened. "That's okay. I know the fire chief in the next town. We can question him. He'd have some insight if anything was found to identify the owner."

"You know," Cassie said, "we sent Robert off with Missy."

"Yeah, we'll clear him first as he's the logical person. He has full access to Missy."

Cassie's phone rang and she answered through the Bluetooth speaker. "Hi, Levi."

"Hello, sweetheart."

JD gritted his teeth at the greeting. He had to control his jealousy. He remembered what Cassie's jealousy had done to their relationship, and he wouldn't allow it to happen to them again.

"I'll be in at ten p.m. in New Orleans."

"Do you need me to pick you up?" Cassie asked.

"No, I'll stay in a hotel, then drive over in the morning. Then, we'll get busy."

Yes, they would. I'm tired of running in circles on this case.

"See you in the morning," Cassie said and ended the call.

That bit of jealousy still prevailed, no matter his desire. He needed to marry this woman, and fast. It was time for another talk with his son. He had to come around because this marriage would happen, at one point or another.

Chapter Twenty-Seven

Sullenly, JD drove home. He'd hoped Cassie would come with him, but she'd wanted to prepare her mother for Levi's visit. He didn't consider her match-making the most brilliant thing, but he'd support her to the ends of the earth.

Cece met him at the house with Henry Kyle. He liked his son spending time with his aunt. It was good for him to have that link to his mother.

"Hi, Cece. Was he good?" JD asked as she met them on the front porch.

She nodded and smiled. "Of course. He's always good."

Henry Kyle hugged his aunt and rushed into the house with a "Hi, Dad" on the way.

JD shook his head. Gaming, online chatting, and cell phones have ruined this generation. He might have to lay down the law with his son on how many hours he could spend online. For now, the boy didn't abuse the time.

"Same time tomorrow?" JD asked Cece.

"Yes. Thanks for letting me watch him," she replied. "It means a lot."

JD knew it reminded her of her sister—JD's ex, who was murdered not long ago. "Anytime. He loves spending time with you. But, Cece—"

"Yes?" she asked.

"—quit spoiling him so."

She shook her head and laughed. "Never."

They said their goodbyes, and JD went hunting for his son. They needed to discuss this marriage thing again. He would marry Cassie. Henry Kyle needed to get on board.

"Henry Kyle!" JD hollered from the living room.

His son poked his head into the room. "Yes, Dad?"

"Come here, champ."

With a loud sigh, Henry Kyle slid into the room, the headphones around his neck with loud music playing. Cooper slinked in behind his son as if he'd also been summoned. As expected, the kitten came trotting along behind Cooper, tripping over her feet as she attempted to yawn and walk simultaneously.

JD liked how the cats and his son had bonded. A kid needed a pet, even though JD had expected a dog. He mentally shrugged. He didn't expect to like the fur balls as much as he did.

Back on topic, JD said, "First, turn down the music. You'll go deaf."

Henry Kyle rolled his eyes and clicked off the headphones. He stood, waiting for the following command, not looking too pleased about it.

"Second, sit down. We need to talk."

Dropping onto the couch, Henry Kyle said, "Again?" Then he patted his leg and Cooper jumped up on his lap. His son petted the cat and smiled. Phoebe, not to be forgotten, crawled her way up Henry Kyle's jeans to his lap.

"I want to talk about my marrying Cassie."

Henry Kyle slumped and looked down. "I don't need a new momma."

JD narrowed his eyes. "Look at me when I'm talking to you." How many times had he heard that growing up? Too many to count. "I don't want to marry her so you can have another mother. I want her to be my wife so we can always be together. Wouldn't you like more time with Miss Cassie?"

Shrugging, Henry Kyle said, "I guess."

This was going in a different direction than JD wanted. He wanted his son's approval, not that he needed it to marry Cassie. But it would benefit his son's and Cassie's relationship.

"Then why are you against my marrying her?"

His son shrugged again. Boy, how JD was beginning to hate that movement.

"I don't want a new momma," Henry Kyle repeated.

"I understand, but she wouldn't be taking your mom's place. She'd be augmenting it." Yeah, that probably sounded corny to a kid. He had to find a better way to explain how great it would be to have Cassie around all the time.

After a brief silence, Henry Kyle said, "I like it here with just you and me."

JD's heart swelled with love for his son. "I like it here with just the two of us, but I also like it with the three of us. Don't you enjoy times with Miss Cassie?"

That sullen shrug again from his son almost drove JD over the edge. "Do whatever you want, Dad."

Had JD been that flippant with his old man growing up? Probably. Oh, how he disliked it coming from his son. "Here's the thing. I will marry Cassie, with or without your blessing. I'd love your blessing, and knowing you'd welcome her to the family."

Henry Kyle jumped up from the couch, the cats screeching as they fell to the floor. "I don't need another mom!" He ran to his room and slammed the door.

JD sat there, dumbfounded. "Well, that went well," he told the stunned cats.

He'd give his son some time and discuss the topic with the psychiatrist about this change. Maybe he was going about it all wrong.

In the kitchen, JD pulled out rice, tomato sauce, a jar of canned tomatoes he'd bought at the farmer's market, spices, left-over rotisserie chicken, sausage, shrimp, and prepared holy trinity. They'd have jambalaya tonight. It'd been a while since they had a good Cajun meal. JD had it when he temporarily lived with Gus and Nan.

As JD and Henry Kyle ate dinner, JD tried to prod something—anything from his son. The boy had turned into the monosyllable king.

"Why don't you want me to marry Miss Cassie?"

Henry Kyle gave an aggrieved sigh. "I told you, Dad. I don't want a new mother."

"What do you think a mother is?"

"Well," Henry Kyle said and pushed his bowl aside having picked out pieces of onion, "Mom told me to do stuff all the time. She wouldn't let me do things with other boys and wasn't fun at all."

It was JD's turn to sigh. He hated that he'd lost that time with his son. If Susan hadn't tried hiding from JD, Henry Kyle's life might have been different. "You know, Miss Cassie isn't like your mom."

Henry Kyle picked up his fork and began to twirl it between his hands. "I know."

"Then why the pushback?"

"I don't know. I just like it like it is."

"I do too, champ. But it's time for our lives to progress. Both of ours. We deserve to have someone else share life with us. She won't take away from what you and I have together. That's two different kinds of love."

"Really?" Henry Kyle's eyes widened. "How?"

Oh boy, did he really need to have this conversation while his son was so young? He'd heard kids did things younger these days, but not this young. "Well," JD started, pushing his empty bowl away, "there's the love between father and son. It's a bond that can never be broken." He almost choked on the words, remembering his old man and their shitty bond. "It's a different kind of love than a man and woman. A strong independent man can have both in his heart."

"Hmm," Henry Kyle said, now twirling the fork between his fingers like a baton. JD wanted to snatch it from him.

"Will she tell me what to do all the time?"

Duh, of course. "She'll tell you when you need to be reminded, yes. So will I."

"Do I have to call her mom?"

That broke JD's heart. He knew Henry Kyle wouldn't call Cassie mother initially, but he hoped he did at some point.

"No, you don't."

"What if you have kids with her? Will you still want me?"

Ah, the crux of the problem has finally spilled out.

"Why would you think I'd not want you, champ? You're the best thing that has happened in my life."

Henry Kyle shrugged again. "I dunno. I just heard how other kids got a new mom or dad and had new kids and didn't get any more attention."

JD wondered where he'd heard it since he'd always been homeschooled but didn't ask.

Scooting his chair closer to his son, JD put his arm around Henry Kyle's shoulder and a hand stilled the spinning fork. "Champ, you'll always be my firstborn and hold a special place in my heart. If Miss Cassie and I have kids, they'd just enhance our family. Wouldn't you like to have a younger brother or sister?"

"No. I like it like it is." He sounded like a broken recording.

"But wouldn't a younger brother or sister be fun to play with?"

"I dunno."

JD wanted to scream. "I dunno" and shrugs were driving him crazy. "Well, it could happen, even if Miss Cassie and I aren't married." Not that JD would allow it, but his son didn't need to know about wearing condoms right now.

"Really?" His son's eyes widened. "How?"

No. No. No. He was not having this conversation. "Let's get back to having Miss Cassie as my wife. What do you say? Wouldn't you like her here every morning and evening?"

"Would we still get to do things without her, like sail?"

JD smiled. "Yes, but I think we'd have to take her sometimes. She loves the boat too."

Henry Kyle frowned. "What about new kids? Would they come?"

Oh boy. "It depends on their age. But, I promise, at

times, just you and I will go." JD would keep that promise if it killed him. His son was too precious to him as was their relationship.

The fork stilled, and Henry Kyle looked him in the eyes. "Promise?"

JD nodded. "Promise."

"What about brothers and sisters? Do I have to have them?"

"Not right away." He hoped. "But I'm sure we'd want children at some point." He really needed to chat with Cassie about that part of their future together.

"I don't know, Dad."

"I think you'd make a great big brother."

Henry Kyle's eyes widened. "I would be the big brother, wouldn't I? I can tell them what to do, like leave me alone."

That wasn't what JD meant, but he wouldn't argue if his son liked the idea. "Pretty much, but I hope you won't want them to leave you alone."

"But they'll be babies," Henry Kyle whined.

"Only at first."

"Do I still get to keep my room?"

JD hoped he could hold up to this. "I don't see why not."

Henry Kyle thought for a moment, then nodded. "Okay, Dad. You can marry her."

Chapter Twenty-Eight

Levi arrived at Coastal Investigation bright and early. Cassie went to the door when she heard the shells crunch, warning of a visitor. She and Levi hugged, and she heard JD clear his throat. *Really?* How could he be jealous of her and this older man?

"Levi," Cassie said, "I'd like to introduce you to JD Walker. JD, this is Levi I've been speaking with at the FBI."

JD extended his hand, and the men shook with "Good to meet you" chorused.

Levi spotted Daisy. "Now, who is this beautiful woman?"

Cassie almost rolled her eyes at his blatant flirtation. "Levi, this is Daisy Kelly. She keeps things running around here."

Daisy briefly looked at Cassie and smiled. Cassie couldn't remember ever saying something so pleasant about her to anyone. Not that she'd said nasty things—she'd avoided saying anything for the most part.

"Nice to meet you, beautiful flower," Levi said.

This time, Cassie did roll her eyes.

Sitting at her desk, Daisy raised her hand to shake, but Levi pulled it to his mouth, giving her hand a small kiss.

JD groaned loudly, and Cassie snickered.

"Who this be? Some *couyon*?" Gus asked as he

entered the primary office.

"Not crazy," Levi responded. He reached Gus and extended his hand. "I'm Levi Bronson."

Nan smiled. "It's about time we got some expert help around here. I hear you're good with computers and finding things."

Levi nodded. "Not to toot my horn too much, but yeah, I'm pretty good."

"Get busy, *couyon*," Gus said.

Cassie wondered if Gus would continue using that term for Levi. He wasn't foolish or crazy, but men used it liberally. "Let me show you around," Cassie said.

After a quick tour of the small building, Cassie and Levi sat with the team at the conference table.

"Okay," Nan said. "The FBI has cut us off."

Levi cleared his throat.

Nan smiled at him. "Officially. But Missy wants us to help find this killer since it appears to be one of her beta readers. Now, we're returning to tricky areas that might get us in trouble."

JD grunted. "Not like we haven't before."

Nan nodded. "True, but this time McKay is after you, JD. He'll flip his lid if he knows Levi is helping us."

Levi raised a hand as if answering the teacher's question. "Will it help that as far as I know, McKay doesn't know me. I've never helped on one of his cases."

Everyone smiled. "That work," Gus said with a huge grin.

It was good to see the older man smiling again. Cassie had worried about his health, but he appeared fine now.

"All right, let's find out who this Alex Finley really is." Nan pointed at an empty desk. "Levi, you can work there. Let me know what you need, and we'll provide it."

"All I need is an internet connection. I can do the rest," Levi said.

The morning went fast, and when Cassie's stomach began to protest, she stopped and asked the team about lunch. Daisy ordered them sandwiches and drinks.

Over lunch, Cassie asked Levi, "How goes it?"

After swallowing his food, Levi said, "It's going. I need to get through a few more firewalls for information."

"Any ideas who it is?" JD asked between sips of his drink.

Levi halted the sandwich to his mouth. "Some. But I need to confirm because it's too easy."

"What do you mean too easy?" Daisy asked.

"I mean, it's been too easy to find the information I've been seeking."

"Well," Cassie said, "you do have FBI access."

"That's the thing," Levi replied, "they've got a ton of data no one is sifting through. It's like they're not rushing to close this case."

"Well," Daisy said, "the final murder has occurred, so they're not expecting anything more."

"True." Levi took a sip of his drink. "I'll find our needle in the haystack."

Nan and Gus entered the room and sat to eat their sandwiches.

Nan said, "I hear from Cassie you're retiring soon, Levi."

He looked over at Cassie and raised a brow.

With her mouth full, she smiled and shrugged.

"I am at retirement, but I can stay longer if I choose."

"Well," Gus said, "choose us."

Cassie stopped. Did they offer Levi a job? That would be awesome. They needed a techie, and Levi was one of the best.

"Excuse me?" Levi asked.

Nan took over. "We were about to post the job for another team member. We've wanted to hire someone with computer experience. I know it's soon, but you've helped us before, and Cassie speaks highly of you, so we'd like to offer you a job on our team. We can't meet your FBI salary at this stage in your career, but the cost of living is so much cheaper here, you won't notice the difference."

"Plus," Cassie piped up on the "Hire Levi" train, "you'll also have your retirement. It's great here. We could work together again, doing something good."

Levi raised a hand in protest. "Okay, okay. I'll consider it."

Gus nodded. "Do that, *couyon*."

"Okay, but if I do, you have to stop calling me that," Levi told Gus.

Gus smiled. "No can do."

There was light laughter amongst the group at the table. Even Levi joined in on Gus's jesting with him.

Cassie hoped Levi chose to work with them. It'd be a bit like old times. They'd been on separate teams in the FBI but worked closely together on several cases.

After lunch, they returned to work, each going through any evidence or link they could find. JD approached her in the late afternoon and slid a hip on the corner of her desk. "How about sailing this weekend?"

Caught off guard, Cassie looked up from the computer and shrugged. "Sure. Can we invite Levi if he's still here?" She could tell by the change in JD's expression that it was a "No."

"This is for you and me, alone. It's been a while since we've done that."

"What about Henry Kyle?" she asked.

"Cece wants to take him to the aquarium this weekend."

"Did she find a place to live?"

JD nodded. "She's coming back to her cottage. She never sold it."

"Smart woman," Cassie said. One day soon she needed to find a place of her own, but things were nice at her mother's. Plus, she was being allowed to save up the down payment.

"Well, hot damn!" Levi shouted.

Cassie and JD turned to look at him, waiting.

Levi turned around. "Let's get the team together."

Cassie liked how he called it "the team" as if he were already a member. "You got something?" she asked.

Shrugging, Levi stood and then stretched with his arms over his head. "Yes and no."

Well, they'd take it for now.

Chapter Twenty-Nine

"So," Levi said, "as we know, Alex Finley is an alias. A few years ago, the real Alex Finley died in a car crash. Our culprit grabbed his info and bought the house—with cash, mind you—before the death was in the government system. There are no records of Alex Finley past that except that the land taxes were paid each year."

"How did this person earn a living?" Daisy asked.

"Using his true identity," JD said.

"So, you've narrowed it down to a male?" Cassie asked, knowing they'd done that since they didn't believe a woman could have overpowered and moved the victims as much as had been with each crime scene.

Levi nodded. "A male purchased the property, so yes, I'm going with male."

"For the big question," Nan said, "do you know who it is?"

Levi stretched his neck, circling it around. "Not yet. But I think it's someone close to the case or Missy."

Cassie straightened, worrying about her friend. "What makes you say that?"

"The knowledge of what is happening—" Levi picked up a piece of paper in plastic from the table and turned it around. "Remember the note and knowing the FBI was involved? That was before our involvement became public. Plus, the timing of our fake Alex's home burning is very suspicious."

Cassie slumped. They hadn't gotten anywhere except confirming their suspicions. Except that the person was close to the case. Did that make it Robert or Carl? What about Agent Angler? Cassie discounted Agent Miles since she was a woman. Then, her heart dropped into her stomach. Could it be Mike? Levi did say the FBI wasn't processing all the information as it should have. Mike could have dual lives that no one would know about.

No. She mentally shook her head. That was stupid. It couldn't be Mike. She never should have gone there. So, if it was someone close, then who?

"How sure are you that it's someone close to Missy or the investigation, Levi?" JD asked Cassie's burning question.

Levi shrugged. "I don't have any data pointing that way. It's just a hunch. A big hunch."

Well, we've worked with big hunches before. Cassie looked at the time. It was almost seven o'clock. Time had flown. She didn't want to wait to find the killer, but they had to eat and rest.

"How about we find this person first thing in the morning?" Nan suggested.

Well, if the boss suggested it, Cassie wouldn't argue.

"Works for me," Levi said. "I'm starved."

Cassie looked at all the bags of junk food and chips littering Levi's temporary desk and shook her head in laughter. Knowing her mom had made her famous lasagna, Cassie invited JD to dinner.

JD nodded. "I don't see why not. Henry Kyle is

already there since your mom homeschooled today."

After the team said their goodnights, Cassie and Levi, followed by JD, traveled to Cassie's mom's home. She relied on her hunch that her mom and Levi would get along. Her mom needed love, and so did Levi.

"I hope the couch is okay. I've heard it's incredible to sleep on," Cassie said, now a little nervous about the introduction.

Levi waved away her concern. "I've slept on worse. Besides, it'll be nice to have company instead of staring at the TV in a hotel room."

That helped to ease Cassie's apprehension about the sleeping situation.

When they arrived at Patricia's, Cassie took a deep breath and released it slowly. If there was no spark, then there was no spark. They could also become good friends. Or nothing at all, a small piece of her mind said.

"Here we are," Cassie told him as she turned off the Jeep.

"It's lovely," Levi said. He turned to Cassie. "Quit worrying. You're worrying about something. Quit. The case can wait one more day."

She smiled at him. The wrong worry, but she was worrying. She hadn't played matchmaker since college, which hadn't worked out so well.

JD opened Cassie's door. "Let's go, children. I can smell that lasagna from here."

Cassie and Levi chuckled and exited the vehicle. Before they reached the door, Henry Kyle appeared. "Dad, Miss Pat cooked lasagna. Can we stay, please?"

"Sure thing, champ." JD ruffled the boy's hair on

the way inside the house.

"Da-ad." Henry Kyle dragged out the word, fixing his hair to its normal messy state.

Patricia met them as they entered the living room. "Hello." She extended her hand to Levi and smiled. "You must be the incredible Levi I've heard so much about."

True to Levi's personality for flirting, he picked up Patricia's hand and kissed it. "I thought I was meeting Cassie's mother, not her sister."

Patricia smiled and shook her head. "I'm Patricia, but you can call me Pat."

Still holding her hand, Levi said, "*Enchante.*"

Cassie thought she'd vomit at the over display of—well, whatever men thought it was when they did something that dramatic.

Yet, Cassie's mom blushed. She truly blushed. Then playfully swatted at Levi. "Oh boy, you're going to be a handful."

Levi grinned widely.

JD broke into the heavy flirting with, "Is dinner ready? We're starved."

Patricia and Levi broke eye contact. *That's good. They appear to be taken with each other, even if it is just sex appeal.* Cassie's spirits rose.

"It's been ready for an hour. You worked late today."

They nodded and followed her to the dining room. "Sit," Patricia said, "I'll get the lasagna from the warming pan."

"I'll help," Cassie said, following her mom from the room.

When they were in the kitchen grabbing the salad,

bread, and lasagna, Cassie whispered, "Well?"

Patricia looked confused and whispered back, "Well, what, dear?"

Frustrated, Cassie mumbled, "You know. Levi?"

Patricia smiled a bit wistfully and said, "Oh, he seems nice." Then, in her average voice, she told Cassie, "Now, don't forget to grab the salad tongs." Her mother carried the steaming lasagna from the kitchen to the dining room, leaving Cassie with the question still in her mind.

It's too early to tell if anything sparks with them. Be patient. Ha, patience was the one thing she lacked in spades.

Cassie noticed JD left the two spots on each side of her mom open so she and Levi could sit there.

That turned out fantastic as she noticed her mom and Levi's hands touch for a bit longer than necessary to pass something. *Yes!* She wanted to fist pump.

After an extremely long dinner where everyone pulled back from the table patting their full bellies, Levi said, "This has been the best meal I've ever had."

"For that, you get to take the single serving of lasagna left over for lunch tomorrow."

Levi's grin broadened. "Winner, winner, chicken dinner."

The adults laughed, and Henry Kyle shook his head. "That's old."

"Well, champ," JD said, "so are we." He ruffled his son's head and laughed when Henry Kyle slipped from under it, fixing his hair.

"Let me help clean up," Levi said.

"I'd appreciate that," Patricia said.

Cassie started. Had her mom accepted help from a

guest? That was a big no-no in the Southern world of etiquette. But it sounded good to Cassie. The two could get to know each other.

In the living room, with JD and Henry Kyle, Cassie turned to JD. "What do you think?"

Turning from the video game he and his son were playing, JD asked, "About what?"

Cassie wanted to yank the game controller, but her mom had given it to Henry Kyle to play after he finished his schoolwork, and for father and son to bond.

Fidgeting, Cassie stood and headed to the kitchen.

JD's arm snaked out while still looking at the screen. "Leave them alone."

She flopped back down, wanting to know what had the two laughing so in the kitchen.

"They're adults. They'll be fine," JD told her. He leaned over and kissed her on the cheek. "Now, help me with the game. This kid is whipping my butt."

Cassie was engrossed in pointing out perils to JD in the game when her mother and Levi entered the room.

"We're going to take a walk. Does anyone want to join us?" Patricia asked.

When Cassie went to move, JD said, "No, enjoy yourselves. Just be home by curfew, children."

"Ha, ha," Levi said with a wink. He turned his gaze toward Patricia. "I think she's worth breaking curfew."

Once they were gone, Cassie noticed Henry Kyle elbow his father and whisper. JD shook his head. "Not now."

Cassie wondered what "not now" meant but left it. It was time to beat a kid at a video game the young one had mastered.

Chapter Thirty

McKay found out about Levi visiting and helping Coastal Investigation. He made it known by dropping in on the CI office. He and his two henchmen FBI agents arrived first thing in the morning to warn, no, threaten Levi for interfering in an investigation.

JD had a feeling the asshole had someone watching Cassie. Why couldn't McKay leave things alone? *Well, because we men don't like to lose, now do we?*

Throughout McKay's tirade, no one said a word. Everyone sat like little scolded children. JD worried for Levi's FBI future. Once McKay left, his toadies following in his wake, the CI team looked at Levi.

Levi looked around. "Oh me," he said. "Well, I thought about it last night, and I think we need to interview the agent and journalist."

"Levi," Cassie said, "you could get fired for helping us. We don't want that."

Waving off her concern, Levi said, "He's full of himself. I don't expect he realizes how valued I am compared to him."

JD's eyebrows rose. What? The prodigal son not valued as he thought. That pleased JD to no end.

"What we're trying to say," JD said, even though he was the least articulate of the group in these situations, "we want you working here, but not because you've been fired from the FBI, of all places."

Levi shook his head. "I won't get fired. Now, about these interviews?"

"What makes you think of these two? I mean," Cassie said, "we've wondered if it is someone close but hadn't even considered Carl."

"Well, he's a writer, isn't he?" Levi said. "Why wouldn't he want to be a beta reader for a well-known author? His words and thoughts are being published in another medium."

"But," Daisy said hesitantly, "what about the love part of the note Missy received?"

"That tells us the person is either sick or knows her enough to fall in love." Levi turned to Gus and Nan. "Don't you agree?"

"That he be sick? Yeah, *couyon*," Gus said.

Nan grimaced. "We know he's sick. And it is someone impersonating Alex Finley." She looked around and everyone nodded. "I say we go back to square one and read the note again."

Cassie quickly pulled it up on her phone and read it out loud.

After she finished the recitation, JD wanted to hit something. This sick fuck was on the street and possibly had been at the table with them, laughing at their inability to solve this case. "I don't like the 'so many more wrongs to right in the world' part."

"How about liking none of it," Cassie said.

Well, there was that.

"We're getting nowhere." JD stretched his neck. "Before we start questioning the two nearest Missy right now, tell us why you chose them and not others."

"Oh, I have another," Levi said, narrowing his eyes at the door. "But, let's pool together what we have and go from there. We need to track some people's whereabouts and that'll take me logging in where I shouldn't while on vacation. So, we need to make it worth it."

JD's gut clenched. He liked Levi. The guy was witty yet sharp and knew his stuff. Plus, he and Cassie were good friends. While it made him jealous occasionally, he knew nothing would come of their relationship. And she needed friends. She hadn't connected with any since she'd returned, except Missy. And look how that's gone.

"Cards on the table," Levi said. "Let's start with Robert, the agent. What have you got?"

"He watches her closely and caters to her every whim," Cassie said.

Daisy said, "He's always touching her, like covering and patting her hand to stop her from worrying or putting his arm around her to comfort her."

"Have you ever noticed how jealous that makes Carl?" Nan asked.

"Okay, so they both like Missy. That doesn't make them a killer," JD said, although he'd bet the killer was close to her also. "I'm not real keen on Agent Angler. He's followed us when McKay says he didn't send him."

Levi nodded. "I have him on my radar also."

Cassie hesitantly asked, "What about Mike?"

The room became silent for a minute before Levi said, "I doubt it's him."

JD knew those were famous last words, but he also didn't consider McKay to be their killer. An asshole, yes. A killer, probably not.

Nan sighed. "This is why we need you, Levi. We

can question them, and track some things, but we can't trace them. That takes a techie expert."

"I will find this fake Alex Finley for you. I recommend you get out there and watch our suspects today and see what you can glean of their activities now that they're waiting to have Missy fall in love with him. Then, we question them."

JD and Cassie took Carl, while Nan and Gus took Robert. Daisy asked if she could tag along, and as much as JD wanted to be alone with Cassie, he allowed it. It turned out Daisy wished to become an investigator once she finished college.

From the backseat of JD's truck, Daisy asked, "Why aren't we just questioning them now?"

"Because," Cassie said, "Levi needs time to get us something to question them about. We can't just ask if they're in love with Missy and expect them to say 'Yes, I'm the killer.'"

"Oh."

JD looked at her in the rear-view mirror. "We do much surveillance, so you'll have to get used to it. People's habits say a lot about them."

They pulled to a curb in Carl's neighborhood. He lived in a nice house for a journalist, but then again, he had been a national correspondent at some point and not a local paper boy.

"What do we do now?" Daisy asked.

"We wait," JD said.

"What if he doesn't leave?" Daisy asked.

"Then," Cassie said, "we wait longer. At least until Levi tells us he has something."

When Carl stepped outside his home, got into his Lexus, and headed to Biloxi, JD had an idea. He turned to Cassie as he started the truck. "Call Missy. See if she's seeing Carl today. Please find out more about when the next article on her will be done. And doesn't Robert have more clients?"

Cassie nodded and made the call. She spoke quietly while JD followed Carl through the sparse traffic. Not easy to hide, but it was the most traveled route out of town.

After finishing the call, Cassie turned to face JD and Daisy. "Missy is seeing both Robert and Carl today. She was slightly suspicious of me asking about them, but I put her off."

"We're going to have to bring her in at some point," JD said.

Cassie waved her hand. "I know, but I don't want her to act differently around either of them. Anyhow, the set of articles is complete, just waiting for their scheduled printing. Carl has convinced her to allow him to hang around until after the killer is caught so he can be the one to grab the scoop."

All JD could think was *damn reporters.*

"What about Robert?" Daisy asked.

"Well, he does have other clients, and the agency he works for is getting a bit irate at his staying at Missy's side. He says he needs to be there until Carl is gone because he doesn't trust reporters."

Neither did they.

They needed Missy away from the men. "Call her back and ask her if the two of you can spend the day together—alone."

After a quick call, Cassie said, "She's waiting for us to pick her up. She sounded relieved. I'm guessing she's tired of the two men fawning all over her."

"Let's get her to CI and see what we can find out about these two men from the woman one supposedly loves," JD said.

Arriving at the hotel, Missy stepped through the front door on their arrival and slid into the front of the truck—Cassie having moved to the back seat with Daisy.

"Thanks for the break," she said. Seeing everyone in the truck, she sighed. "This is just a Cassie and I day, is it?"

"Nope," JD said. "We need to chat without your two hounds in attendance."

As they pulled onto the highway, JD saw the nondescript car pull out to follow. While he couldn't tell exactly who it was, he could tell it was only one person. He doubted McKay would sit in a car waiting, but he wouldn't put it past Agent Angler.

Well, they had nothing to hide. They were going back to work and had their client in tow. The FBI can't do a thing about the situation.

"What do we need to chat about?" Missy asked.

"We're going to find a killer," Daisy said way too excited.

JD would have to work with her on speaking with a client. But he likes her exuberance in the task. "We have some questions we think you can answer."

"I don't know who the killer is," Missy said.

"No," Cassie said. "We believe you. But you may know something to help us find him."

"I'll do what I can."

Arriving at CI, JD saw an excited Levi and a smiling Nan and Gus. Had they figured out the killer? He certainly hoped so. He was tired of feeling inadequate in a case. They'd done nothing but go around in circles, it seemed.

Once everyone sat, Levi said, "I have a plan."

Stiffening, JD didn't know what to say. That was his line. He was the one on the team who came up with plans to catch a killer now that Gus had semi-retired. If they hired Levi, he'd have to learn this. His job would be to help find the bad guy or girl, and JD's job would be to capture them, either in the act or in general.

"What is it?" Missy asked.

"You're getting married tomorrow," Levi announced.

Taken aback, Missy asked, "To whom am I suddenly marrying?"

With a broad smile, Levi pointed his thumb at his chest. "Me."

Chapter Thirty-One

"Why are we doing this again?" Missy asked Cassie as they settled on the sofas in the hotel suite living room.

Cassie also thought it an outlandish idea, but she'd try anything. "Well, because if you're suddenly marrying someone who is not 'your ardent fan' then he will let himself be known, somehow. And, as for it being Levi, well, he's not known by the others, so it could be a whirlwind romance."

"I don't see how it will work."

They hoped the killer would do more than write a note this time. That he'd confront Missy about the marriage and his supposed love for her. That was why Cassie would stay with Missy without anyone else the wiser.

It seemed a bit far-fetched, but they didn't have another option to try at this point. They figured out who the fake Alex Finley was by sorting through tax records at the Louisiana home. He'd paid with a personal check the first year, and his name was recorded on the receipt before he started paying cash. He'd done an excellent job of otherwise covering his trail.

Now, he needed to act. JD and Daisy were on night surveillance, while Nan and Gus would take day surveillance, if necessary. Levi watched the computer for electronic moves their killer took.

"Why don't we just tell the FBI you've figured it out?" Missy asked.

Because, while it was petty, they didn't want Mike to get credit for the takedown, and because Mike probably wouldn't believe them and have Levi fired. "They won't believe us. Besides, we're acting for you. If you don't want to do this, just say the word."

Missy shook her head. "No, I'm fine with it. It's exciting but a bit nerve-racking. Do you really believe he'll come to my hotel room?"

Cassie blew out a breath. "I don't know." She bit her lip briefly before adding, "But we believe he'll confront you somehow, and we haven't given him time to see you anyplace else."

Missy nodded. "That makes sense." She visibly shivered. "I still can't believe he's been here all this time."

At a knock on the door, Cassie put a finger to her lips. If it were their killer, then JD and Daisy, little help as she was, would not be far behind.

"Just a minute," Missy said.

Cassie worried about her friend's mental health, so on her way to the second bedroom, she whispered, "You've got this. I'm right here when you need me." She didn't say "if" because Missy would need her.

As Cassie settled into the second bedroom, with the door ajar enough that she could see in the living room, Missy answered the door.

"Robert," Missy said. "What are you doing here?"

Robert? Cassie left the bedroom to join the arguing she heard from Robert and Missy.

"Children," Cassie said, stopping the two. "What's going on?"

Robert seemed put out that Cassie was there, but straightened and said, "I can't manage someone who doesn't confide in me about their plans."

Did he mean catching a killer? No. No. He couldn't know. "What plans?" Cassie asked.

"This marriage," Robert almost spit out. "And, to a nobody."

"He's not a nobody," Missy argued, as if the relationship were real.

Cassie appreciated Missy getting in character, but enough was enough. "Robert, you need to leave. You can discuss this in the morning."

It took a minute, but the two women returned Robert to the door. As Cassie swung it open, she received another surprise. *What was this? Grand Central Station?* They'd never catch their killer if they couldn't get Missy alone.

"Mike," Cassie said. "What are you doing here?"

"What are you doing here?" he asked back.

Indignant, she replied, "I'm Missy's friend."

Mike nodded at Robert, whom Missy nearly shoved out the door.

"May I come in?" Mike asked Missy.

Missy looked at Cassie, who briefly shook her head. "Now is not a good time," Missy told Mike.

"I wasn't really asking," he said as he pushed by her.

Asshat. Cassie shut the door behind him, but not before looking down the empty hallway. They had to get Mike out of here, and fast. "What's so important?" Cassie pressed.

"I've relieved Agent Angler of his duties. I had no idea he wasn't doing his job. All kinds of evidence haven't been processed. For that," he spoke to Missy, "I'm sorry."

"What do you mean?" Missy asked.

"We'll get it all sorted in the morning. Until then, I'd like to put a detail on you."

"There's no need for that," Cassie said. "She's got us if she needs protection."

Another knock on the door and Cassie rolled her eyes–so much for a plan. No one else seemed to adhere to it. "I'll get it."

Looking out the peephole, adrenaline spiked, and her heart went into overtime. *He was finally here.* They weren't ready. But backup had to be close.

Undoing the snap on her holster, she slowly opened the door with her hand on the butt of her gun. What she hadn't seen through the peephole had pure fear skittering up her spine.

Brandishing a gun, he waved it at Cassie to open the door. "I figured I'd find you here. A final girl's night before the wedding?"

Cassie lifted her hands near her head. The gun had a silencer. *Who the hell got silencers today?* Apparently, killers did.

"Turn around," Carl instructed.

She knew better, but she would be a wall between herself and her friend. So, she turned, and Carl reached around and caught her by the neck, nearly choking her. She imagined that was the point. With his gun pointed at her back, she stood stiffly, facing the room.

"Cassie?" Mike hesitantly asked.

"Here's your killer," she responded as she walked into the living room, never taking her eyes off Missy. She heard Mike's gun leave the holster. *A bit late, buddy.*

"Drop the weapon," Mike demanded, moving around the room. He moved in front of Missy, quietly telling her to "get down." *Thank you, God.*

"Don't count on it," Carl said as he remained behind Cassie to keep Mike from having an open shot. "Put your gun down, or your ex gets it. I've killed before, and I'll kill now."

"No can do."

What? Cassie wanted to strangle Mike, even though she knew their job was to protect Missy. She wanted to scream, "Shoot this asshat, *now!*". Where was JD? "Mike?" She heard the wobble in her voice. *Strength,* she reminded herself.

Mike barely shook his head, signaling he didn't have a shot. Her gut was tangled in knots. She was not going to die at the hands of this maniac. JD would save her. They had a solid plan, and he'd arrive any minute and sneak up behind Carl, bringing this show to a halt.

"Missy and I are leaving here together," Carl said. "I won't let her marry someone else. I've gone through too much to prove my love to her. I know she loves me for it."

"Alex Finley," Cassie said.

"You figured it out, did you? Too bad it won't help you."

"Is that what you think?" Cassie asked, trying to stall for time.

Ignoring her question, Carl said, "Missy, I know you love me as much as I love you. Don't marry this other guy. Marry me. We'll be great together."

"You're not taking her anywhere," Mike said.

"Missy, don't make me shoot your best friend,"

Carl said, moving them slowly around the room. "I will if you don't come out from behind McKay and leave with me."

Missy began to stand.

Cassie shouted, "Missy, no!"

Thankfully, her friend ducked back down behind Mike. "But I don't want him to shoot you."

"Don't worry, Missy. Do you remember the plan?"

"What the fuck are you talking about, Cassie?" Mike asked, but his attention never left Carl.

Where the hell is JD? He should have been here by now. Something must be wrong, or Carl gave him the slip. Since Cassie knew that no one gave JD the slip, JD or Daisy must be injured. Cassie's throat strangled at the thought. She wouldn't allow this crazy man to continue to ruin her friend's life, especially if he'd wrecked hers by hurting JD.

She elbowed him, but his hold around her neck only tightened.

He shoved the gun deeper into her back. "Don't push me, bitch. I'll kill you and lover boy to get what I want. Only, I don't want my Missy to see me kill you. That is, unless she doesn't do as I say."

Cassie couldn't believe that Carl had fooled them so easily. The man was a raving lunatic. He was a maniacal killer, not the soft-spoken journalist they'd come to know.

"Carl," Missy said, "please don't do this. Don't hurt these good people."

"Now we're getting somewhere," Carl spat. "Come out, and let's go."

"If I do, will you let them go?" Missy asked.

Cassie prayed her friend was stalling so the cavalry

could arrive and not considering going with this asshat. However, she knew that Missy was like her—she'd do anything to protect those she loved. Anything.

"Missy, no," Cassie repeated.

"Cassie," Missy said, standing, "I can't let him kill you and even your asshole of an ex-husband."

"Thanks," Mike muttered, his laser focus on Carl.

"See," Carl said, "Missy is a brilliant woman. My woman. Come to me, sweetheart, and I'll let Cassie go."

"No can do," Mike said. "She stays behind me."

"Then, you'll die," Carl warned.

"Cassie," Mike warned, "get out of the way so I can shoot this fucker."

So, she dropped, leaving Carl attempting to manage dead weight. Unable to manage her with one arm, she slipped from his hold and did as JD had taught her—to pull her weapon on the fly. During those few seconds, she heard two shots, one muffled, the other filling the air. She held her gun on Carl and watched the red pool around his heart as he crumpled to the ground. She quickly stood and kicked his handgun away from him, holding her unfired gun on him. "Missy? Mike?" she called.

The door flew open, and Cassie pointed her still-drawn weapon toward it.

"Whoa," JD said, "it's just me."

"Where the hell were you?" she asked with true anger in her voice. He was her backup, and he hadn't been there. She'd had to rely on Mike, of all people.

JD surveyed the scene. "Someone, I suspect Carl, had hotel security set on me for carrying a weapon. It took a lot of talking to escape another asshole."

JD looked out the doorway. "It's clear." He knelt and felt for a pulse on Carl's throat. "He's dead."

At those words, a wide-eyed Daisy stepped into the room.

"Cassie," Missy said. "Mike's been hit. I'm on with 911."

Oh no. She rushed over to Mike and dropped to her knees. His right side was covered in blood–a lot of blood. "How bad is it?" she stupidly asked as she began to apply pressure on the wound.

Mike hissed as she pushed down. "I'm not going to die if that's your wish."

Cassie shook her head. "I don't want you to die. I want you to leave me alone. Let me live in peace with the man I love."

"You loved me once," Mike said between gasps of pain.

"Yeah, well, you crushed that love, Mike."

Cassie felt a hand on her shoulder, and JD handed her a T-shirt, the one he'd been wearing. She held it to the wound. "Tell me about Agent Angler," she said, trying to change the subject. "You were telling us you'd pulled him earlier."

"Oh," Mike said, "he wanted to close the case, so when I came in and overrode him, he countermanded anything he could to discredit me, so he could come in and save the day."

"Well," Cassie said, "you showed him, didn't you? You caught the killer and received a wound in the battle." She felt JD's hand tighten on her shoulder. Yes, she'd just given the credit to her ex-husband, but by gosh, he'd been shot trying to save them. He could have died. Well, in truth, so could she have. Carl could have come in shooting, but he only wanted to talk to Missy, it seemed.

Mike grasped Cassie's arm. "I never deserved you."

Now Mike talked like he was dying. That worried her as the wound didn't seem that severe unless it had lacerated something internal. All she knew was that it was bleeding heavily, even with her staunching the flow of blood.

"No, you didn't," JD said.

Mike looked past her at JD. "You take care of her. She's one special lady."

"I will," JD said as the room swarmed with the fire department, cops, and paramedics.

"We've got him," Cassie was told by one firefighter whom she knew to be an EMT also.

She grimaced because she wasn't ready to pick up her hands. "Take care, Mike." With that, she lifted herself and turned him over to the professionals.

Chapter Thirty-Two

Spending the evening in the emergency surgical waiting room hadn't been JD's idea, but he'd support Cassie, even in this. She assured him she didn't have feelings left for McKay, but he had been shot saving Missy.

And the fucker did pull through. Now, JD owed McKay for Cassie's life, which rankled in his crawl. He hoped the man never came to collect.

The bright spot had been that Cassie hadn't wanted to see McKay after the surgery. She'd just wanted to know he pulled through. Cassie said she couldn't handle someone dying to save her life.

As JD dropped her back at her Jeep, still at the hotel, he had a thought. Now wasn't the time, but maybe it was. He leaned over to her, putting his arm on the back of the seat, slowly massaging her neck.

"Hmm." She closed her eyes. "That feels wonderful."

"Let's take a quick walk on the beach. The fresh air will do us both good."

Opening her eyes and looking at him, she nodded. "That does sound refreshing."

They exited his truck and jaywalked across Highway 90 to the beach. Kicking off their shoes, they jumped in the sand like children. They quietly walked, hand-in-hand, to the waterfront, only stopping to roll up their pant legs.

"What was that favor you asked of Carl? I never did hear."

JD shook his head. "He was to get my complaint about McKay to the right desk, but it turned out he didn't have any contacts."

"Oh," Cassie said. Then, as if they'd not had the conversation, she said, "I love living near the beach."

JD nuzzled her neck. "I love living near you."

"Mmm, that does make this the best beach in the world."

JD held her tightly. "It nearly killed me when I heard gunshots coming down the hallway and knowing you were in there." He wasn't sure he could handle her being an investigator when it would jeopardize her life. And that was almost always because you couldn't account for what a crazy person would do in every situation.

"I was fine." She kissed his neck. "I had Mike at my back."

Wrong words. It dumped ice water on the walk. He pulled back, keeping his arms around her, only loosely. "What do you want to do about him?"

She scrunched up her brows. "What do you mean?"

"Do we report his behavior or not?"

Cassie bit her lip, and he knew the turmoil within her. The man could have died saving her life. Does she destroy his career or let it go? "I say we let it go for now. If he pops up again, then things will be different."

Jealously welled in him. She'd had years with McKay. Years he hadn't.

"I'd rather not talk about Mike," she said, pulling him down for a kiss. "I'd rather talk about this." She pressed her lips to his again. JD invested all the passion he felt for Cassie into the movement of his lips over hers.

After they came up for air, JD said, "Let's continue walking." He needed to or he'd take her right here in public. And he wasn't for public nudity or an audience to their lovemaking.

"Sure."

They untangled themselves and continued down the beach, with Cassie playing in the waves crashing on the shore. JD laughed at her antics of jumping over each one and getting splashed each time. Oh, how he loved this woman.

Now didn't get much better. They both loved the beach, and they were alone, except for the traffic on the highway. JD stopped them.

"What's wrong?" Cassie asked as they stepped on the dry sand.

"Nothing is wrong. In fact, everything is right."

"Okay. Are we headed home?"

"Home is something I want to talk with you about." He held his breath for a moment and dropped to one knee. He'd practiced with Henry Kyle, who'd laughed at him, and hoped he remembered what he'd wanted to say. No one told him he'd be this nervous.

JD pulled the box from his pocket that he'd been carrying for the right moment. "Cassie—"

"Oh my God," Cassie interrupted, covering her cheeks with her hands.

"No, it's just me." JD grinned at her and opened the box to display the two-carat, princess-cut diamond ring surrounded by small sapphires. "I've loved you most of my life. The years we had apart left me empty inside. I'm glad to have you back in my life. But I can't do this part-time thing. Henry Kyle and I have talked. We want you for my wife and his stepmother." There, he'd gotten most of it out. Oh yeah, he forgot the part about buying the house with her in mind. Oh well.

She dropped to her knees. "Are you sure? Both of you?"

He pulled the ring from the box. "Yes. We discussed it at length." JD wanted to roll his eyes to the degree he'd gone to discuss it with his son, but this wasn't the right moment. It was too serious.

"I'm not sure I'm ready to be a stepmother."

His heart cracked. What if she didn't accept? He hadn't thought of that scenario and what he'd say. "Sure you are. You're great with him."

"I'd like a kid or two of our own," she said as if negotiating with him.

"That sounds good. What else?"

"I'd like a nice wedding. I didn't have one before because I didn't want it. Now, I want the world to know we're tying the knot."

Did she just agree? "Are you saying you accept?"

She threw her arms around his neck. "Of course! I love you, JD Walker."

"And without a doubt, I love you, Cassie McKay— soon to be Walker."

He leaned over and kissed her. Once they broke apart, he placed the ring on her finger. Thank goodness Patricia had known the right size. "Should we tell our son?"

"*Our* son? Wow, that sounds so… I don't know, exciting. I love that kid."

"He loves you, too."

They stood and walked back to the hotel, this time arm-in-arm. At the hotel, they decided to leave the Jeep and take the truck home together. Cassie seemed lost in thought, and that worried him.

He reached over and clasped her hand. "What's the matter? You're not questioning your decision, are you?" *Please don't be questioning it.* He'd finally gotten the "yes" he'd wanted since high school.

"I was thinking of a beach wedding."

JD liked that idea, although he worried about rain. They'd figure it out when the time came. He'd leave all that stuff to her. Didn't women expect to plan that with their friends and mothers?

When they arrived at Cassie's mom's home, Henry Kyle came running out before JD could exit his truck. "I was getting worried. Mr. Levi said you wrapped up the case hours ago."

"Back up, champ, so I can get out of the truck."

Henry Kyle did so. When JD exited, his son whispered, "Did you ask her?"

JD nodded.

His son's eyes widened. "And what did she say?"

"I said yes," Cassie said, coming around the side of the truck. She joined JD and their hands locked.

"Yay!" Henry Kyle whooped. "Dad said he'd have two of us to give him gray hair."

Cassie glanced over at JD. "He did, did he?"

"Yes, and he said we'd drive him to an early grave," Henry Kyle went on as they walked to the front door.

"Champ, stop before she changes her mind."

"Hey, you two," Patricia said. "We were getting a bit worried. Levi's been here for hours."

"We have news," JD said. Since he'd already confided in Patricia, she glanced down at Cassie's right hand. "Oh?"

"You knew?" Cassie asked.

"Of course. Your mother always knows."

They walked into the living room. "What does a mother always know?" Levi asked.

Cassie held out her left hand, displaying her ring. "We're getting married."

Hugs went all around, and JD stood back watching Cassie and her mom make plans.

Levi patted him on the shoulder. "You couldn't have picked a better woman."

JD quirked an eyebrow. "Oh yeah?" He looked at Patricia.

"Well, the perfect woman for you." Levi chuckled.

"So, anything between you and Pat?" JD asked.

Levi cocked his head as he watched her laugh with her daughter. "I don't know. But, I plan to remain here to find out."

"Does this mean you're taking the job?"

"Yes."

"Great," JD said, "because I believe Cassie has something to ask you." He talked louder to address Cassie. "Honey, didn't you want to talk with Levi?"

Her eyes brightened. "Oh, yes." She came nearer. "Levi, would you give me away at my wedding?"

JD could have sworn Levi's eyes watered, but as a man, he'd never point that out.

"Of course, kiddo."

All was right in JD's world. *Now, I just have to survive the wedding planning.*

A Note from Sheila

Thank you for reading *Read Between the Lines*! If you enjoyed reading Cassie and JD's continued story, I would appreciate it if you would help others enjoy this book, too. You can recommend it to friends, readers' groups, and discussion boards. It will mean a great deal to me if you'd take a moment to write a review and share how you feel about my story so others may find my work. Honest reviews help bring my books to the attention of other readers. The best news is that only a few words are needed.

A word about the author…

Sheila Kell writes about romantic men who leave women's hearts pounding with a happily ever after built on memorable, adrenaline-pumping stories. Her debut novel, *His Desire* (HIS Series #1), launched as an Amazon #1 romantic suspense bestseller, later winning the Readers' Favorite award for best romantic suspense novel.

As a Southern girl who has left behind her days with the United States Air Force and as a University Vice President, she can usually be found in South Mississippi, where she lives with her cats and all the strays that magically find her front door. When she isn't writing, you can find Sheila with her nose in a good book, dealing with the woodland critters who enjoy her backyard, or wishing she had a genie to do her bidding.

Ways to connect

SheilaKell.com

facebook.com/sheilakellbooks

instagram.com/sheilakellbooks

goodreads.com/sheilakellbooks

bookbub.com/authors/sheila-kell

I'd love to hear directly from you. Please feel free to email me at sheila@sheilakell.com.

Don't miss out on new releases, exclusive excerpts, and giveaways!

Join my newsletter www.SheilaKell.com/subscribe